Colleen

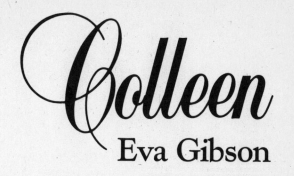

Colleen

Eva Gibson

BETHANY HOUSE PUBLISHERS

MINNEAPOLIS, MINNESOTA 55438

A Division of Bethany Fellowship, Inc.

Colleen
Eva Gibson

Library of Congress Catalog Card Number 85-70561

ISBN 0-87123-809-8

Published by Bethany House Publishers
A Division of Bethany Fellowship, Inc.
6820 Auto Club Road, Minneapolis, Minnesota 55438

Printed in the United States of America

To my Mother,
Jenny Nickerson,
who taught me as a child to love the Shepherd

EVA GIBSON, a homemaker with six children, is active in a Baptist church in Sherwood, Oregon. She is a free-lance writer whose articles have been published in several youth periodicals. She has written three other novels in the Bethany House Publishers line.

Table of Contents

1 / Storm. 9

2 / And After That the Dawn. 18

3 / Hedged In 25

4 / Stranger From the Sea 34

5 / A Blend of Fantasy. 41

6 / The Mouse 48

7 / The Black Diary 55

8 / Follow the Moonpath 64

9 / Elusive Paths. 72

10 / More Than a Love Story 79

11 / The Shepherd of the Sea. 88

12 / A New Day Dawns. 95

13 / Silver Paths 104

14 / Secret of the Sun. 112

15 / The Moon Pendant 121

16 / Rainbow Wings. 131

17 / The Stones Cry Out .140

18 / A Pendant and a Promise 151

1 / Storm

The storm began with pushing and prodding against the wide window facing the sea. I carefully blended the pink reflection of my painted sunrise and put down my brush. Pressing my nose against the cold glass, I watched the rushing waves rise higher and higher.

The wind teased the waves into curling tufts and tossed bits of foam onto the beach. A strange yellow glow illuminated the stunted spruce jutting from the cliff.

The sea, the wind, the luminous light stirred me. I *had* to feel nature's fierce abandon.

Pushing the brush into the cleaner, I caught up my hooded blue jacket and zippered it snugly, leaving the hood to sail over my shoulders. I wanted to run against the wind and feel it push through my hair.

As I ran toward the beach, sand stung my cheeks and made my eyes water. Crashing waves and wind screamed around me.

Pausing, I watched a sea gull trying vainly to fly a straight course. His feathers were rumpled and he was low—too low. For a moment I thought I saw panic in his tiny eyes.

"Keep going!" I yelled, my voice faint against the noise of the storm. "Find a safe harbor!"

I turned inland.

It was then I realized this was no usual storm. As I turned, a tree toppled from the bank above my house, branches sailing through the air. The big birch tree tumbled into the side yard and lay quivering.

Suddenly a huge wave crashed in on me from behind, sending me off balance. I grabbed a massive stump embedded in the sand and hung on while the sea rolled around me, intent on sucking me oceanward. Then with a great rush the wave receded. Like a piece of giant seaweed, I curled around the stump.

My numbed fingers released their grip and I ran toward the house. As in a dream I saw the roof roll back and fly into the air. Horror crashed in on me.

My painting—the one of my sister and me running in the pink sunrise—I had to rescue it before the waves and rain destroyed it.

"Oh, God . . ." I prayed. I ran frantically toward the house, the wind around me snatching my breath. My wet jeans clung like ice from some freak silver thaw, hampering my steps.

The sound of splintering glass battered my ears as I shoved open the door. I drew back as shattered fragments slammed against the walls.

"My picture!" I screamed. I started to run to it but a man's voice jerked me back.

"You fool! You'll be cut to bits in there!"

I turned around. The man ran toward me as more glass fragments flew through the air like sharpened swords bent on destruction. My knees gave way and I stumbled against the porch rail. He bounded up the steps, caught my shoulder and turned me seaward.

Even in my fear and weakness, the strength and beauty in those charging waves pulled at me. *Like white-maned horses*, I thought. *No. Like God, majestic, powerful*.

The man took my hand and pulled me down the steps. "I'll take you to safety!" he cried. "Trust me."

I had no choice. My house was in shambles—the waves and sea had turned against me. I let him pull me away.

He strode ahead, dragging me when my own knees threatened to give way. *Should I be doing this?* I wondered, *following a stranger?* Dimly I realized his strength, the broadness of his shoulders.

He turned his head and I saw rivulets running down his brown beard. An alder crashed in front of us and lay trembling, its green leaves still tortured by the wind.

He released my hand and parted the branches of the

fallen tree. I climbed through, my own limbs trembling more than the tree's. A white Toyota pickup was just beyond. He went to it, opening the door on the passenger side.

As he boosted me inside, I felt like a small child. The door slammed shut, muting the storm. I covered my face with my hands.

The stranger opened the door across from me, springing inside. "Don't be afraid," he said. "We're as safe here as anywhere, right now."

I uncovered my face and looked at him, noting his straight nose and jutting brows. His dark brown corduroy coat was soaked, as was his brown hair. I noticed the V-shaped crease between his eyes, the gentleness and concern in their hazel depths. *He's younger than I thought, maybe twenty-five* . . .

Quite suddenly I was conscious of my own appearance. My blond hair straggled over my shoulders and my face, devoid of makeup, was wet from the waves.

I rubbed the back of my hand across my nose and wished desperately for a tissue, or better yet, a towel.

He leaned across me and opened the glove compartment. I took the Kleenex gratefully and wiped my nose. "Thanks."

I shoved the box back inside and looked out the window. Trees twisted in the wind, sending debris and branches flying in all directions. Steel gray clouds raced across the sky.

The pickup shuddered, partly from the force of the wind, partly from the response of the motor. We backed out slowly, then turned toward the town.

Rain and wind lashed at the houses. I saw a toppled tool shed and more downed trees. A huge piece of shining tin sailed down the street in front of us.

"This is unreal!" I gasped. "I can't believe it's happening."

"It *is* unreal," the man agreed. "I've never seen anything like it. I just pray that no one is injured or killed."

I shuddered. "*I* could have been. That flying glass . . ."

He stared straight ahead, intent on guiding us safely through the storm. "Why? Why did you do it? Go back inside . . ."

His question pierced into my heart. "It was my paintings," I whispered. "They're all I have right now. And the house belongs to Pete. It's all he has—and he's been so good to me."

We turned into the parking lot of the little white church I attended. "You'll be safe here," the man said. "Come."

I scrambled out, my knees feeling like damp putty as the wind caught at me.

"It's more protected here!" the stranger shouted. He grabbed my hand and propelled me toward the church door. The double doors opened and I was inside.

Strangers and people I knew surged around me. Sherry, my minister's wife, was holding two-year-old Jonathan. But that didn't stop her from putting her free arm around me and giving me a welcoming squeeze.

"My house," I said, "it's gone." My voice caught. "My paintings—"

The tightening of her arm around my shoulders was her answer. After a moment she slipped away.

I moved toward the far end of the foyer and looked across at the parsonage. The fence encircling it was flattened. The tall beautiful birch tree I'd always enjoyed lay horizontal, its roots exposed, its top sticking through the parsonage's bay window. I shivered as I thought of splintered glass flying relentlessly through the air in my own tiny house by the sea.

But here inside the church the big double doors held the storm at bay. "Daddy's out there," whispered a voice beside me.

I looked across at Sherry's daughter, Tiffany. She came close and I saw fear mirrored in her dark eyes. I reached out and touched her soft brown hair, then rubbed her cheek.

"You're cold," she said. "Were you outside very long?"

I nodded. "I went down to the waves."

She touched my wet jeans. "I can tell. Is your house still there?"

I swallowed hard. "No." I whispered. "The roof blew off and the windows are broken."

She tilted her head and looked at me. Her brown eyes,

so like Sherry's, rested on me with trouble in their depths, mirroring her concern. "Will you go home now?" she asked.

I took a deep breath. "I don't know, Tiffany. I just don't know."

My thoughts battered me as I stared out at the raging wind. Home—my sister Melissa, Mom, Dad, Darryl. They wanted me back. What idiotic stubbornness made me resist their love? Why was I here alone in a small windswept town with only my paintings for company?

Tears filled my eyes as I visualized my sunrise painting mutilated by piercing glass, made sodden with slanting rain. But it wasn't just the painting. It was my past that tore at my insides.

My dreams and my freedom seemed empty and selfish. *And it's my running away that's done it.*

Strange, that hadn't bothered me until my sister had found me. Ever since the morning Melissa had left me alone on the beach and waved good-bye, I'd felt my old restlessness returning.

I had stood there, a cold lump of unexpected homesickness welling up inside my throat. "Oh, Melissa, Melissa," I had whispered.

My hand had come up to hide the quivering of my lips. When the car faded into the distance, I turned and went into the house, doubts tearing at me.

They were tearing at me now. Only this time it was coupled with remorse.

I'm Colleen Lloyd, I thought, *twenty years old—old enough to know the direction I'm going. But I don't.*

A tin chimney toppled by the wind rolled past the window. *Like me, torn from its place, tumbling around and around.*

"That's Mrs. Delker's chimney!" Tiffany exclaimed. She turned her round-eyed gaze toward me. "Is this really happening?"

I understood what she meant. The force of the wind was awesome, the destruction unreal.

Tiffany and I stood together, mostly without words, and

watched the wind tear and stab and twist. After a while it began to die down and evening wrapped itself around the shattered town.

Gradually the men drifted into the building, excitedly sharing bits of information. Tiffany's anxious eyes stayed glued on the double doors. I could see hope leap every time they opened.

When her father came, Tiffany grabbed at him, clinging to his shoulders, burying her heart-shaped face down into his jacket.

One hand came around and stroked her soft brown hair. "Why, honey," he said. "It's all right." He sat down next to the window and gathered her into his lap.

Her long legs dangled over his, but it seemed neither incongruent nor odd. A lump formed in my throat. What would it be like to be twelve again and held tight in a father's arms?

Jack's blue eyes met mine over the top of Tiffany's head. "Most of the houses are safe, Colleen," he said gently. "But yours—well—it was too close to the water."

I swallowed hard. "I know," I said. "Did you go down there?"

He nodded. "The roof is gone and the windows let in the sea. I'm sorry."

I lowered my eyes so he couldn't see my misery, but he seemed to know how I felt. He said, "I have a place for you to live, Colleen. There's an elderly lady in our church— Opal Standby. She sits toward the back when she comes, and I don't know if you've noticed her."

I shook my head.

"She's needed someone for a long time. I'd like you to stay with her—if you would."

I tried to keep the bitterness out of my voice. "I guess I don't have a choice."

"Yes, you do," he said gently. "You can stay with Sherry and me for a while. We're your friends, Colleen. No—family, if you'll have us."

Sherry came into the foyer, Jonathan's legs still wrapped

around her waist. *She must be exhausted,* I thought, *hanging onto that child for so many hours.*

She sank to the floor beside her husband's chair and rested her head against his knee. "The electricity will be out for several hours, Jack. If I had our camp stove here, I could make a great pot of stew."

Jack rested his hand against her cheek for a brief intimate moment. I turned my head away, feeling like an intruder in the precious family moment. But Sherry smiled at me, an open wide smile that had all the marks of friendship woven in it.

"Want to help me cook stew?" she asked. "I'll need all the help I can get cutting enough vegies to feed this crowd." She waved her hand around the room.

"Of course," I said.

Jack stood up still holding tight to Tiffany's hand. "Come with Tiffany and me to our garage," he said. "I'll need an extra hand." Tiffany reached for my hand.

"Bring all the stew fixings you can find," Sherry called after us.

We went out the side door, our hands welded together against the elements. The wind against our faces was strangely warm. It pushed my hair with almost gentle fingers. I looked around anxiously.

Shingles from the back of the house littered the lawn. A ladder sprawled on its side, cast down by the wind. Newspaper mingled with pieces of black plastic lay tangled in the roots of the fallen birch tree, shoved there by the wind's clever fingers.

"It's a mess, isn't it?" Jack sighed. "But no lives were lost—as far as we know."

He opened the garage door and we went inside. He and Tiffany began searching through boxes for the camp stove while I went inside to raid the refrigerator.

Window glass covered the linoleum and it seemed odd to feel wind inside a kitchen, and stranger yet to open a refrigerator and be greeted with darkness.

I peered into its depths uncertainly. *Did one use cabbage*

in stew? I wondered. *Well, they will in this one.*

I dumped the large head into a paper bag and reached for a plastic bag of carrots. I hesitated about opening the freezer compartment and decided against it. Canned vegetables would do just as well as frozen, and would allow the cold to stay in the freezer until electric power was restored.

I added seasonings from the shelf and then a sack of rice, remembering how my mother often tossed in a handful to "make it more filling." A bottle of catsup completed the supply.

Loaded with my contributions, I rejoined Jack and Tiffany. Jack had the stove in one hand and a bottle of propane fuel in the other. Tiffany held up a sack of potatoes.

"See!" she exclaimed. "Potatoes and stew go together!"

I smiled at her, enjoying the picture she made. Armed with her potato sack, her eyes flashing, her head held high, she was a conquering hero. My fingers itched to put down the stew makings and reach for a sketchbook. But of course there was none in reach—nor would there be, considering the shape of my house.

Pushing my negative thoughts aside, I concentrated instead on toting the brown paper bag across the lawn and through the side door of the church. I followed Jack into the church kitchen.

Sherry started unloading as soon as I set my bag on the table. "Oh, good," she said. "Jack loves chunks of cabbage thrown in."

"My mother puts in rice," I said, "and a dollop of catsup."

"Sounds yummy."

She handed me a knife. I picked up a carrot and began to scrape.

Dusk was beginning to fall and I was grateful for the kerosene lantern someone had hung from the ceiling. Already it cast our shadows onto the wall. I could see myself, huge and unreal, crouching over the table. I brandished the knife and the shadow swooped across the wall. Tiffany laughed with delight and little Jonathan chortled.

"You look like the giant in *Jack and the Beanstalk*," Sherry said. "Only he never followed Jack to earth. Tell me, Colleen, how did you get here from your house?"

Startled, I laid the knife down. "There was a man," I said slowly, "someone I'd never seen before. He insisted I leave the house."

Sherry looked at me curiously. "I wonder if he's someone I know. What did he look like?"

"Tall, broad. He had a brown beard." I waited for recognition to flash in Sherry's eyes, but she merely shook her head.

I laid the carrot down. "Sherry, I never even told him thank you. I just—just—took him for granted."

Sherry's brown eyes flashed with amusement. "I doubt if he felt he was being taken advantage of. Most men relish the idea of rescuing a fair maiden in distress."

"A fair maiden, maybe," I spluttered. "This was just me! I'm going to see if I can find him, Sherry. He might be here. And he was so kind, so helpful, while I was so rude!"

I rushed from the room. I needed to find the stranger—the one with hazel eyes and pointy beard, the one who had said, "I'll take you to safety—trust me."

2 / And After That the Dawn

I dashed from the kitchen. Mr. McCalister, Ruddy Hill, and old Ted Hilstrom were huddled together around a lantern in the foyer. They looked at me kindly, a gentle questioning in Ted's eyes.

"Looking for someone, Colleen?" he asked.

I nodded. "The man who brought me from the beach. Did you see him?"

Ruddy Hill shook his head. "Sorry. I just got here." He looked at the other two men. "Know who she's talking about?"

The men looked at me with probing eyes. I felt suddenly awkward and ill at ease.

"I—I don't know his name," I stammered. "He brought me from my house when it was being blown to bits."

Old Ted rubbed his hands together. "What's he look like?"

"Brown beard." I made pointy motions with my hands. "His eyes were hazel, I think. And he was tall—over six foot. About twenty-five."

But the men only shook their heads. "I'm sorry, Colleen," Mr. McCalister said regretfully. "We haven't seen anyone who fits that description."

"Is there anyone in the sanctuary?" I opened the door and peered into emptiness. The darkness and silence mocked me.

Leaving the men, I hurried down the hall. Perhaps in the fireside room . . . But it, too, was empty. I turned away, disappointed.

"I couldn't find anyone who's seen him," I said as I rejoined Sherry at the sink.

"Don't worry," Sherry comforted. "In a town this size he's bound to show up."

"Not if he's just passing through," I lamented. I picked up a carrot and began to cut it into golden pennies. "If only I hadn't been so wrapped up in me, I'd have thanked him and found out his name."

"Maybe he'll return," Sherry comforted.

I nodded and bent over the stew pot.

Supper that night was a subdued affair. The town, still shrouded in darkness, lay quiet and brooding without electricity. But candles blossomed on the long table in the church, vying with the lantern light to lend their own special cheer.

A spirit of quiet determination dominated the conversation. Trees had toppled and roofs had been ripped off, but no one had been hurt in our vicinity. Tomorrow would be a time to rebuild—to reach out to those less fortunate.

The tiny portable radio in the center of the table fed information. The storm was described as the tail of a hurricane, an unusual happening for the Pacific Northwest. It had lashed northward, finally blowing itself out.

Reports of injuries and damages were given out as the radio station received them. In the nearby town of Elsworth a small boy had been killed, pinned beneath a falling tree. Further inland a trailer house had toppled, taking the lives of an elderly couple and their dog. News briefs from Salem and Portland told of widespread destruction.

The radio said no lives were lost in those two cities, but I wondered. *My family—had they been protected by the woods? Or had those majestic firs uprooted, tossed headlong across their shingled roof?*

After the meal was over, Jack offered a prayer of thanksgiving for the protection of the families in our town. "But, Lord," he concluded, "we're thinking of those who have suffered injury—irreplaceable loss. Lord, we ask you to help and comfort them, and show us what we can do."

I could see them in my mind: the parents of the little boy grieving over a tiny, still body, others waiting in a hospital room holding out for words of hope. Then into my thoughts flashed the man who had rescued me from my splintering house, leading me away from the waves. Was he safe? Warm? Comfortable? Would I ever see him again?

I didn't know who he was—but God did. *Lord, I think that man knows you.* The conviction grew inside me that he did—much better than I.

He needs your protection right now. I lift him to you, asking you to put your strong, powerful arms around him. And, Lord, if you could just tell him "thank you" from me . . .

I lifted my head, suddenly aware that Jack's "Amen" had already been said. People milled around me. A child cried dully. Jack's hand touched my shoulder.

"Will people sleep here?" I asked.

"A few. Those who can will be returning to their homes. What about you, Colleen? Would you be content to roll up in a sleeping bag with us here at the church? I'm afraid the wind's blowing too freely through our house."

"I appreciate your offer," I said earnestly. And I did. The only thing that bothered me right then was the dampness of my blue jeans. At first I hadn't paid much attention. But now they were making me chilled and uncomfortable. I longed for a hot shower, my long flannel nightgown, my dark blue bathrobe.

Sherry brought me a white baptismal gown. "Put this on," she advised. She laid a plaid bathrobe over my arm. "And this, too. The shepherds and wise men won't mind."

I smiled ruefully. "They won't," I agreed, "but what about the gown? Won't wearing it be sacrilegious?"

But Sherry only laughed. "You've forgotten," she said, "King David ate the temple bread when he was fleeing from his enemies. I think God is honored when we use special objects to meet other's needs."

I undressed by flickering lantern light in the restroom and joined the others in the fireside room. Jack had climbed up to make certain that the chimney was still intact, and a fire now burned softly, pushing back the shadows and murmuring comfort.

B

3.95

Colleen

Tiffany, Jonathan, Sherry, Jack and another youthful couple whose roof was gone, gathered close around it. Jack opened his Bible and read the twenty-third Psalm, his voice mingling with the fire's.

Something tender and loving reached out to me, hearing about the Shepherd and His sheep—the way He cared for them, led them.

I looked down at little Jonathan asleep in his mother's arms, and saw Tiffany push as close to her father as she could get. *Families,* I thought, *supporting each other, needing each other, accepting one another.*

Oh, why am I so perverse? Always struggling against those I love?

That night I tossed restlessly. In my dreams I was running . . . running . . . always running . . . searching for someone. Was it my mother? Melissa? Or the stranger?

Time and again I dreamed and awoke, then slept again. In the early predawn I awoke again, weary and depressed. Had the storm lashed my parents' home? Were they all right?

Sitting, I pushed back my sleeping bag. Jonathan had sprawled close to me during the night and I edged carefully past him.

I slipped into the restroom and touched the light switch. Elation filled me as golden light blossomed. I turned on the faucet, rejoicing in the gush of warm water. After I washed my face I dressed in yesterday's jeans, then went into the kitchen.

The mass of dirty silverware piled in the sink beckoned my attention. But first I had to go outside. It was several blocks from the beach, but I needed to be there before the sun arose.

Stillness slid around me as I opened the big front double doors. I hesitated, caught by its contrast to the wild winds of the day before. It was hard to visualize that the last time I'd opened those doors, fierce winds had clawed and pushed, driving me forward with almost unreal strength.

The evidence of destruction was all around. Branches torn from trees, lumber tossed askew, and trees . . . A willow across the street had been thrust down in its old age. It lay beside a young firethorn rudely pushed against a house, exposed roots jutting from the moist brown earth.

I thought of Melissa. Trees meant to her what the ocean did to me.

I turned and ran down the street.

The sandy beach littered with debris greeted me. I stopped and took a great breath, then walked toward the waves. Far out, tossing, not yet tipped with light from the rising sun, they beckoned. Strange to think that the people-world slept while God's nature-world stirred and moved around me.

A sandpiper raced ahead of me, his tiny feet making patterns on the sand. A sea gull drifted overhead on an unseen air current. Vaguely I wondered if it was the one I'd watched struggling in the storm. If it was, its battle was over. Mine was just beginning.

A distant wave shone with sudden golden light, another and another, and then the entire ocean sparkled with sunshine, reflecting the blue of October skies. Then the sunshine touched me, comforting me, giving me hope.

A cry drifted across the sand. "Colleen! Colleen!"

I turned. A tall young man with tousled blond hair came toward me.

"Pete!" I cried.

As Pete Erickson came close, I saw concern in his deep blue eyes. He caught my hands in his.

"I came from the beach house," he gasped shakily. "I was so afraid I'd find you there, caught under a fallen board—or bleeding, cut by flying glass . . ."

For a brief moment I was in his strong arms, felt the pounding of his heart. Then I disengaged myself and stepped backward.

"How did you know where to find me?"

"After I was sure you weren't in the beach house, I tried to figure out where you'd go. I remembered the church you'd told me about—so I went there." He gestured inland. "Mrs. Mitchell said you were all right—that you'd spent the night with them."

"I got up early," I said apologetically. "I wanted to see the sunrise and last night's damage. I'm sorry about your beach house, Pete. Awfully sorry. Not just for me, but for you."

But the flashing look in Pete's eyes wasn't concern for any lost property. There was something else in his dark blue eyes. I took another step backward and looked down, not knowing what to say.

His next words confirmed my tumbling feelings. "Colleen, when I was searching that shattered mess, those mutilated paintings, I only thought of one thing. What if you had been lying crushed, the life gone out of your body? Colleen——"

"Don't say anything more, Pete," I entreated. "The storm is past. The radio said it blew itself out in southern Washington. And I'm safe—really I am!"

I lifted my eyes to him and saw the longing. Quite suddenly I pitied him. I started to reach out and touch his hand, then let my own drop by my side.

"I have to go back, Pete. I need to help clean up that mess from last night's supper."

"No, you don't," Pete said jealously. "There are other people there and I need you now."

I looked up at him searchingly, suddenly conscious of the deep indentation in his firm chin, his large, expressive mouth. He drew his brows together and I noticed how well shaped they were, how dark when contrasted with his wavy blond hair.

I shook my head, "You don't understand, Pete. Sherry and Jack treated me like their sister last night. Even before that they were always there, showing their love in little ways. The least I can do is wash dishes!"

"Dishes!" Pete echoed. He looked at me intently and abruptly changed the subject. "Colleen, the house is gone for all practical purposes. What will you do now?"

"I don't know."

"I've been thinking—you really ought to go to art school and develop your talent."

"Art school!" I exclaimed. "Pete, be sensible! That takes money, and right now I don't have any!"

"I've been thinking about it quite awhile," Pete persisted. "You could even stay with my sister. She has an apartment in Portland. And with your talent it would be easy for you to find part-time work doing window displays."

"You talk like it's all arranged," I said tartly. "What does your sister say?"

"Sylvia? She thinks it's a great idea."

"I don't," I said softly. "Why, if I wanted to do that I could go home and stay with Mom and Dad. They're close enough to town."

"But this way you'd be on your own. It would give you a chance to create a career, become a person of accomplishment. Sylvia's a real career woman, polished, smooth."

I didn't answer. Instead, I looked beyond him to the white-capped waves dotting the horizon. I heard the wild distant cry of a sea gull, saw a ship breasting the waves moving farther and farther away. A yearning I didn't understand welled up inside.

"What about it, Colleen?" Pete asked, pulling my thoughts inland. "Do you think it might be worth considering?"

"Maybe. And in the meantime the dishes are waiting. I have to go."

Pete didn't try to persuade me to stay. Instead we walked toward the town.

When he reached for my hand I didn't pull away. But I wondered.

Why was the memory of a stranger's voice saying, "Trust me, only trust me," more real than Pete's voice saying, "Colleen, we're in this together"?

3 / Hedged In

Sherry and I were cleaning the kitchen when the telephone rang. We looked at each other in startled joy, then scrambled for the church office.

I stood in the doorway, rubbing wet hands against my pant legs and smiling at Sherry's eagerness as she picked up the receiver. Her rich reddish brown hair tumbled around her shoulders and her brown eyes shone.

She only spoke a few words, then put the receiver down. "It's working! Call your folks, Colleen."

"It's long distance," I protested.

Sherry pushed the phone across the desk toward me. "Go ahead," she urged. "It's what our church is here for."

I picked it up, a strange mixture of eagerness and reluctance clamoring inside me. I dialed, then waited breathlessly for the clear ringing at the other end. Would my family be safe?

I heard Melissa's "hello" faint and far away.

"Melissa!" I cried. "Is everyone all right?"

"Yes! Yes!" At her next words, gladness traveled down the phone line and settled into my heart. "We're fine—except a lot of the trees in the woods out back were uprooted. But what about you, Colleen? We thought of you, prayed for you. That little house is so close to the water!"

"It's gone, Melissa," I said, trying to keep the quiver out of my voice. "The roof blew off."

"Your paintings! Oh, Colleen . . ."

I swallowed hard. "Destroyed. I haven't gone back yet, though. Maybe I can salvage something."

"Poor Pete," Melissa mourned. "How awful. Colleen, will you—"

"Will I what?"

"Come home—now?"

I shook my head. Then aware that she couldn't see me, said, "No. Not yet. I—I can't."

"But where will you live? How will you live?'

I took a deep breath. Up to this point uncertainty had dragged at me. Now I knew what I would do.

"My pastor knows an elderly lady in town who needs a companion. He suggested I apply. At first I wasn't sure, but now—well, I'm going to try it. Somehow—somehow it seems right. Are Mom and Dad there, Melissa? Could I talk to them?"

"They're over at the Thompson's," Melissa said regretfully. "The damage to their house was unbelievable. The top of a fir blew off, then plunged through the kitchen like an arrow."

I gripped the receiver more tightly, and shivered. "Tell them I called, won't you? I should hang up now. I'm at the church—but I wanted so to see if everyone was all right."

"We're fine—fine. Write soon, Colleen. And remember, we love you."

My own "I love you" seemed barely audible.

A lump filled my throat as I put down the receiver and went back to the kitchen. After I'd assured Sherry of my family's safety, I told her what I'd decided.

She nodded. "Jack will be pleased. And so will I. Opal Standby lives only a few blocks from here and we'll be able to see you a lot."

"And," she added, "I think you'll get along famously. She's needed someone like you for a long time."

She carefully wiped the top of the camp stove and clicked it into place. "Colleen, I've needed a friend like you, too."

Her arm came around my shoulder. Once again my throat tightened and I had to fight back tears.

That afternoon Jack and I went to call on Opal Standby. Doubts tumbled through my mind as we drew up in front of a white old-fashioned house behind thick overgrown hedges. I held back, staring uncertainly at the jumbled maze of greenery, untrimmed and uncurbed, rising high above my head. The green leaves of the closely packed bushes formed a dark barrier.

Jack sensed my feelings and smiled reassuringly. "She tells me she can see the sea from the upstairs window. Come on. I think you'll be pleasantly surprised."

Reluctantly I opened the car door and got out. The cement path leading to the front door was cracked, with tufts of grass sticking up here and there.

But I liked the front porch. It went across the entire front of the house. Above it, gabled windows peeked at me and I saw the ruffles of snow-white priscilla curtains.

"Strange," I said. "She's apparently had very little storm damage."

Jack nodded. "She has the wooded hill behind her, and in front those thick overgrown laurels. They cut off a lot of wind."

"I don't like them," I shuddered. "They're menacing."

"But a beautiful spot to shelter small birds, chipmunks. Sometimes—"

He broke off as the branches beside me trembled. I moved closer and started to part the leaves. But before I could peer into the dark depths, a huge yellow dog lunged at me.

"Get back!" Jack cried.

I screamed as the creature broke through the leaves, its teeth bared. Jack's arm shot out, thrusting me aside. I was knocked to my knees. Before I gained my feet, I smelled the wild dog's hair, felt his breath on my cheek. Then he was gone, his great fur-matted legs moving back and forth like pistons—away—away—vanishing into the far end of the hedge.

Jack's hand came down and pulled me to my feet. "Are you all right? Did he bite you?"

Dazedly I shook my head. "Yes, I'm all right. And no, he didn't bite me—I don't think."

I touched my fingers to my face, then examined my knees. "Not a scratch," I said shakily.

"When I said the hedges sheltered wild things, I had no idea," Jack apologized.

"Are you going to tell Miss Standby?" I asked.

"I'm not sure. I hate to put fear into her. And the dog may have just been passing through. What do you think?"

"I don't know." I brushed off my pant legs, then turned as the front door opened.

The loveliest little lady I had ever met stood there, dressed in soft lavender. She peered at us through her silver-rimmed glasses, questions wreathing her wrinkled face.

Lavender—old lace—they just suit her.

Jack stepped onto the porch. "It's Pastor Jack," he said, "come to bring you someone special." He took my arm, patted it encouragingly and propelled me forward.

"Hello, Miss Standby. I'm Colleen Lloyd."

I looked down at her. She looked so frail, and yet somehow strong. I sensed in her a wiry tenacity that belied her appearance and made me hope to be like her someday.

Jack smiled at me over the top of her shining silver hair. "Opal Standby is one of the lovely ladies in our church. She has an eye for beauty, too."

Opal reached out and took my hand. "From what Jack has told me, so do you." She turned my hand in hers, studying it intently. "You have the working fingers of a true artist, my dear. I think we'll get along."

My eye caught Jack's. Without a word we agreed to say nothing of the wild dog who'd hidden in her hedge.

Opal opened the door and we stepped into a room made alive and gracious with firelight, contrasting with the dreary, overcast afternoon. She motioned us toward it and I saw how the glow of the fire gave color to her pale, fine skin. I noticed her hand, small boned, fragile as she rested it on the white marble mantle.

She gestured across the room. The elegance of dainty crocheted doilies decorated couch and chairs. In spite of my recent fear, I let out a little cry of delight. An old pump organ stood in the corner. Tiny Kewpie dolls smiled from the cubby holes on the side.

"This room is beautiful!" I cried. "The decorations—the organ—no wonder Jack said you have an eye for beauty.

You must have an ear for it too!''

Opal stepped over to the organ, resting her hand lovingly on the organ's polished maple surface. ''It's been here as long as I can remember. My sister used to play it—but I never did.''

''Oh, Miss Standby, would you care if I did?''

Opal's gray eyes flashed with memories. ''Ah, if only,'' she said regretfully. ''But it doesn't work. Not anymore.''

''That's all right,'' I reassured. ''Actually I've never played an organ. Just piano—and that was several years ago.''

Slowly we moved through the house. Its half-hidden nooks, window seats and unexpected doors and corners captivated me. Even the steep stairway had a surprise turn— not just one, but two.

A delighted ''ooh'' slipped from my lips as Opal opened the door of the upstairs gable bedroom. ''This will be for your use, dear, if you decide to stay.''

The room was all I had ever dreamed a bedroom should be. The wooden four-poster bed boasted a handmade quilt in an old-fashioned pattern, and small braided rugs studded the shining hardwood floor with patches of color. Even the slanting ceiling had an old-fashioned charm.

My attention was caught by an embroidered verse on the wall opposite the bed. ''The path of the just is as a shining light.''

The words were underscored by a path done in heavy gold stitching, edged with green-gold birch trees. Overhead a golden sun cast light rays.

I went to the window and looked outside. Jack was right. The sea, though distant, beckoned me. A lump swelled up again. I was going to miss my little house by the waves.

I looked down at the maze of overgrown shrubs and felt suddenly depressed. *Dark tunnels . . . wild dogs . . .*

Opal came and stood beside me. Her next words sounded as if she'd heard my thought. ''My mother planted the hedges years ago. She came from the valley and brought with her a deep love for flowers.''

"The hedge is terribly overgrown," I ventured. "Shouldn't you have it removed?"

Opal sighed. "There are lots of memories there that make it hard. The ocean wind made it difficult for Mother to grow her flowers and she got the idea of growing laurels to cut off the wind. Gradually she planted them into little garden rooms. One had a sundial—it's still there behind that birch tree. Another was a rock garden with miniature plants."

She gestured to the far right. "The rose room was over there. And beyond that was her autumn room. I can still remember her golden chrysanthemums and colorful dahlias."

She smiled up at me. "People are like flowers, you know," she said confidentially. "You're something golden, like sunshine—maybe chrysanthemums or daffodils and forsythia."

"It must be my hair," I said awkwardly, running my fingers through its golden blondness. "Friends back home sometimes called me Miss Sunshine—or Sunny."

"It's not just your looks. Even your voice reminds me of liquid sunlight."

"What about Marigold?" Jack asked, his tone amused. "The fragrance is incomparable."

We laughed. "Well, I know which flower you are, anyway," I said to Jack as we went downstairs. "Skunk cabbage. They're big and glorious and golden."

"And very fragrant," Jack and Opal finished for me.

The silly remark made me feel better, pushing back the cloying branches and the memory of the attacking dog. Jack and I were in good spirits when we returned to the car an hour later. I would have dinner with the Mitchells', then return to the gabled house behind the hedges.

I slept that night in the elegant four-poster bed. My dreams were of people with strange faces clad in old-fashioned clothes. One lady in a purple bonnet seemed to have taken a particular fancy to me.

"You've come to the right place, my dear," she said

over and over. Everytime she said it, she'd poke me with a sharp, long-handled stove poker that was somehow transformed into a hat pin when it reached me.

The lady faded into darkness, only to be replaced by smothering laurel. They came closer and closer, towering over me. A dog growled menacingly. When I awoke I was not rested.

Opal and I breakfasted on toast and orange juice. Afterward I felt better. A silly purple-bonneted lady and her host of hedges wasn't going to keep me down.

"I need to go back to my house on the beach," I said as I carried our plates and cups to the sink. "Jack said he'd drive me this morning, but I'd rather walk."

Opal nodded. "Of course, Miss Marigold," she said impishly, cocking her silver eyebrows. "You don't mind if I call you that, do you?"

"Not if I can call you Miss Lavender," I said boldly. "That's what I thought the first time I saw you."

Opal seemed pleased. "That's lovely. I wonder why I never thought of it. Miss Lavender. But of course it wouldn't have fit when I was young."

"What did?" I asked curiously.

But a veil dropped over Opal's open face. "Perhaps someday we'll talk about it," she said quietly.

I didn't pursue the subject. Instead, I zipped up my blue jacket, making myself ready for the three-mile walk down the beach to my demolished house. Opal insisted I take something to eat, so I shoved cheese and bread into a plastic bag and stuffed it into my pocket.

I skirted as far down the hedges as I could, then hurried along the street.

The wind was rising, bringing with it the soft roar of the surf. I noticed the old houses facing me, and a sense of the agelessness of sand and sky and sea reached out and grabbed me. Those houses were young compared to the vastness of God's creation.

The gusts sweeping across the sand welcomed and invigorated me, and I ran toward the sea, laughing at the waves. They galloped toward me like great white horses, then skidded to an uncertain stop before retreating back into the sea.

Back and forth the horses played. A sea gull hung loftily in the sky above me, a painted bird against a painted sky.

"Come and join us!" I shouted. But the gull remained motionless, serene.

After a while I tired of the game and settled into hiking down the coast. The blueness of the sky, the melodic thunder of the waves, and the long expanse of sand worked rest and contentment into my soul. It was true that my life was experiencing change and unrest, but my God who created the universe had everything under control.

The feeling stayed until I entered the bay sheltering my little house. The sight of broken windows and gaping roof broke something inside of me. Discouragement and despair clawed around my spirit.

I had to force myself to open the door and walk inside. Storm-tossed debris was everywhere. Bits of seaweed and driftwood were tangled with the cushions on the floor. My bathrobe lay tossed in a corner, coated with sand.

I picked it up and shook it vigorously. Sand flew. I blinked hard, laid it back down and forced myself to face the paintings that I'd put so much of myself into.

Some of them had been battered by flying glass, still others were blurred and distorted by the water. But the one that had been on the easel—the one of Melissa and me running in the pink sunrise—was gone.

I stared in disbelief at the easel pushed to the floor, then went into the kitchen alcove. Perhaps a freak wind current had torn it from its place, shoved it into a corner.

But all I found was broken china, a sodden corn flakes box, and more shattered glass.

I went to the gaping hole that had been the window and looked out in troubled dismay. Far in the distance, a solitary figure moved away from me, something square tucked beneath one arm. A wild hope leaped inside me.

"Wait!" I cried. The wind tore my words from me and

bounced them back off the walls. I ran through the house and back onto the sand.

"Come back!" I shouted.

But the man was too far in the distance. Before he disappeared from sight I was sure that I recognized the broad shoulders, the long, easy stride.

I knew it was my stranger.

Disappointment closed in around me like an overgrown hedge, shutting out the sun.

4 / Stranger From the Sea

I stood in the garden among battered chrysanthemums and let discouragement press in on me. Why had I told Sherry I would fix the tables for the harvest dinner at church?

When I'd said yes, I'd visualized golden marigolds artfully arranged in vases on the blue and white checkered tablecloths. But Jack Frost had played havoc. The blackened remains of the marigolds mocked me.

"The chrysanthemums will have to take their place," I muttered, brandishing my shears. I began to cut and sort.

When I finished, I looked down at them in triumph. Scarred, windblown, marked with the ravages of November, they were still beautiful, their muted oranges and golds blending into a quiet burst of beauty.

That evening I stepped back to admire my just-finished handiwork. The small vases filled with chrysanthemums on each table were accentuated by bits of fern and tiny sprays of forget-me-nots I found thriving in the protection of Miss Lavender's foreboding hedge. The bouquets looked as attractive as florist creations of roses, baby's breath, and airy greenery.

A light step made me turn. Tiffany smiled up at me, her eyes reflecting varying shades of shadow.

"They're beautiful, Colleen. Like paintings."

I winced.

"I'm sorry," she said. "I didn't mean—I—I forgot about your picture."

"It's all right," I said gently.

"But you seem so sad!" Tiffany exclaimed. "Ever since the storm, and it's been almost a month."

I nodded. "I lost something that day," I admitted. "More than just my paintings."

Tiffany's expressive brown eyes studied me. I knew I needed to explain even though I hardly understood myself.

"I haven't been able to paint, Tiffany. Or draw either. It isn't that I don't want to. It's that I'm almost," my voice lowered, "afraid."

Wonderment echoed in Tiffany's words. "Afraid? To draw?"

"It's . . . it's . . ." I felt myself floundering. "I think it's fear I'll never be able to recapture what I've already done—that nothing I do in the future will be as good."

"I think," Tiffany said earnestly, "if the arts are inside you, they would just come out. Wouldn't they?"

"I don't know." I sighed. "Pete gave me a sketchbook before he went back to the base. But it's so fancy. I don't even want to open it."

Tiffany stepped close to the nearest table. "You just have to start drawing and stop worrying how it will turn out," she said solemnly. "Like you arranged these flowers." She thrust her nose into a bouquet. "These are art."

She drew back suddenly, wrinkling her upturned nose. "Phew! they sort of stink, don't they?"

I laughed. "It all depends on who's doing the smelling. Just as beauty is in the eye of the beholder, so is fragrance in the nose of the sniffer."

Tiffany wasn't interested in my philosophical remarks. She wandered among the tables, admiring the other bouquets.

"Is Miss Standby coming to our dinner?" she asked.

"No. I tried to persuade her but she said she'd rather stay home." I smiled. "She says it's comfortable to just be quiet in the evening, knowing right where her Bible is and being able to sleep over it."

Tiffany nodded and then disappeared down the hall. I sighed and began cleaning up the bits and pieces of broken stems and scattered leaves. I shoved them into a waste can and picked up my jacket.

As I slipped my arms into its warm, fleecy depths, I thought gratefully of the box of clothes my parents had sent down with an obliging friend. It had been fun to dig inside and pull out old familiar friends: the rust and green sweater, last year's jeans, my favorite creamy cardigan.

Melissa, Mom and Dad, and Darryl had all written notes and tucked them into pockets, sleeves and between garments. One was even stuck inside a tennis shoe.

I sighed. Why was my life so complicated? So filled with tattered threads that went nowhere?

"Pete wants me to be a fancy career lady," I muttered. "My family wants me home. What do *I* want?"

I buttoned my coat and opened the door. I zipped across the lawn to the parsonage. My dress for the evening was laid across Tiffany's bed, waiting for me. *Sherry is like a big sister*, I thought, *always trying to help me all she can. I wonder what she thinks*.

The soft ivory folds slid around me, outlining my slim figure. I looked in the mirror critically.

"It needs a touch of color," I murmured.

I saw a movement in the glass and smiled. Tiffany stole softly behind me, her cool hands covering my eyes. "Guess!"

"I saw you in the mirror," I laughed. "Tiffany, come forth!"

She dropped her hands. We smiled at one another's mirror reflections. "I wish I had brought my rust scarf," I lamented. "Knotted under my collar, it would have been just right."

"Wait!" Tiffany cried. She whirled from the room in a circle of deep rose.

She was back in a few minutes, a turquoise scarf with creamy polka dots in her hand. "It's Mother's. She said it was okay."

"Thanks," I said. I arranged it under my collar, then looked intently at my reflection. My eyes looked more blue-green than ever. There was even a luminous quality about my lips, my skin.

Tiffany was delighted. "You look a tiny bit like the waves in that color," she approved. "Let's go."

She took my hand and we went downstairs. Jack's voice

drifted through the open doorway. "We'll have dinner, then our speaker. You'll like Alan, Sherry. He has a way with words, and he's funny, too. Our youth will love him."

Tiffany looked up at me. She wrinkled her nose disdainfully. "Daddy's so sure that everyone's going to like him. But I'm not. I'd rather hear Daddy preach."

"Hush, Tiffany," I entreated. "Your parents would feel bad if they heard you talking like that. After all, your dad did tell me that he's hoping he'll be the new youth pastor, at least through next summer."

As we stepped into the room I couldn't help admiring Jack and Sherry. They made an attractive couple—Jack, tall and blond; Sherry, small, dark, vivacious.

I thought of how good they were, how protecting of me—and Miss Lavender. Jack hadn't wanted her to worry about the dog. Yet he'd alluded to it several times, asking me if I'd seen any trace.

Sherry smiled and held out her hand. "Come on, you two. We'll be late."

The scent of fresh coffee mingled with the good smell of baked bread. The buffet table delighted my eyes—golden acorn squash, baked potatoes with melting cheese, green peas, meat loaf topped with grated carrots and catsup.

"This really is a harvest dinner," I murmured as I sat down beside Tiffany at a table in the center. I leaned back in my chair, examining the flower arrangements for hidden flaws.

My attention was suddenly drawn to a young man seated with the Mitchells at a table across from Tiffany and me. He caught my eye and instantly smiled. A faint electrical current tingled between us. Quickly I averted my gaze to the blue and white tablecloth. My fingers reached up and began to trace the tiny squares.

Tiffany jostled my elbow. "That's him," she whispered.

"Hush, Tiffany," I entreated. "Your whispers are stage whispers. Everyone can hear you."

Covertly I glanced at the man destined as our new youth

pastor. Once again his glance caught mine. I took a quick, short breath. There was something compassionate and caring in his gaze.

I lowered my eyes. He knows how I feel. How can he? I looked up. This time one eye closed in a long, slow wink.

The heat rushed into my face. Had I really thought he understood? He probably was only attracted to my blond hair. How dare he be so brash! And he a pastor—a minister of the gospel!

"He's the one who convinced Daddy to become a minister," Tiffany confided in a low voice. "I don't like him."

I lifted my head, shot her a startled glance. "Don't like him?" I echoed. "But why?"

"Being a pastor is hard. People want so much." Her voice grew louder. "I've heard them say things. They expect a minister and his wife to be perfect. And me too. It's not fair." She flipped a long, rebellious lock of hair behind her shoulder.

"He talked him into it, said Daddy had a pastor's heart. They were in school together."

"Please!" I begged, "I don't like him either. But let's talk later—not now!"

Sudden rose tinted Tiffany's cheeks. She pursed her lips into a petulant pout.

I was glad when Pastor Jack said grace. Afterward we paraded around the laden table. I deliberately concentrated on filling my plate and making small talk with those around me. It was hard to wend back to the table followed by an expectant Tiffany, where I was once again in direct view of the young man with the disturbing wink.

I did very well until Pastor Jack stood and introduced him as Alan Nichols, the man we'd been praying for, our future youth pastor.

Tiffany sniffed. My eyebrows arched. We looked at each other with a note of skepticism, sharing our dislike.

I'm not going to listen to him, I decided. The egotist—thinking I'll fall into his arms at first glance.

I shut out his words by mentally rearranging the blue

forget-me-nots in front of me. But I discounted the power of God's Word.

Alan was reading the twenty-third Psalm, ". . . He prepares a table before me in the presence of my enemies."

He looked at the diners, his hazel eyes intent. "We had a table prepared for us this evening, filled with the bounty of harvest. It wasn't served to us in the presence of enemies, though. It was served in the presence of family and friends.

"Come with me now to Israel—into the wilderness. Let's discover together a path into a green valley. There's a Shepherd there, a fold, a flock of sheep.

"Let's consider our God as the Great Shepherd of a restless, sinning people. The tender Shepherd who longs to feed, provide and protect."

I leaned forward eagerly. No longer did that strange electricity weld our glances together. Something mightier than, bigger than, was drawing us to God.

I let the words of the prophet Ezekiel sink deep into my heart.

"I will seek that which was lost, and bring again that which was driven away, and will bind up that which was broken, and will strengthen that which was sick."

I stood on the lawn outside the church, thoughts of the Shepherd work of the Lord Jesus beating into my heart.

Why am I so afraid to trust such a Shepherd? Why am I always running from His care?

I saw the women through the window, shuffling among the tables, intent on clearing the room, the men clumped together in groups, gesturing and talking. Children circled among them, overflowing into the great outdoors.

A small boy darted past me, disappearing into the shrubbery. Nostalgia tugged at me. What fun to be little, playing a game of hide-and-seek.

Was that what I was doing now? Playing an adult game of hide-and-seek, forever intent on denying my Shepherd's claims on my life?

A tall, dark figure loomed through the shadows—Alan

Nichols. Immediately I forgot the beauty of the Shepherd. I took a step backward. My former disdain nibbled inside me as I remembered only his obvious singling me out in that roomful of people.

"I was so glad to see you here," he said eagerly. "I was looking. Has everything turned out all right?"

I lifted my chin haughtily. "You must think you know me," I said coldly. "But I don't know you."

My iciness startled him. I felt it. An emotion that I couldn't decipher flicked across his face. He lifted his chin and I saw his profile outlined against the gold light from the window.

"Why—I beg your pardon. Excuse me." He turned and strode back into the building.

I put a hand over my mouth. I recognized those broad shoulders, that stride.

It was the stranger from the sea who walked away from me!

5 / A Blend of Fantasy

"That man!" I cried. I unknotted the turquoise scarf from beneath my collar and tossed it on Tiffany's bed. "He's the one!"

"Colleen, you're not making any sense," Sherry entreated. "What man *are* you talking about?"

"The one on the beach who brought me here the day of the storm! It was Alan Nichols!"

A smile played across Sherry's lips. "So what? No harm done."

"That's what you think! Oh, Sherry, I was cold to him. He looked for me and I . . ." I whirled to face her. "He shaved off his beard, didn't he? And I didn't recognize him. But I didn't have to be rude! Oh, I'll never be able to face him!"

"Don't be silly. Jack knows Alan well." Sherry's lips quivered. "When he's had time to realize what happened—what you thought—he'll think it's funny."

But I wasn't sure I wanted to be thought of as a joke. "I was terrible," I lamented. "He'll think I'm an ungrateful wretch with no manners."

Sherry refused to be impressed by my dilemma. "Quit fussing, Colleen. According to Jack, Alan is a real people person, not one to be put off by a silly misunderstanding."

I wasn't convinced. My pride smarted. I dreaded meeting him again.

After Sherry left, I stepped out of my ivory dress and back into comfortable blue jeans.

Tiffany, gentle and confiding in a soft flannel gown, opened the door, one hand clasped behind her back.

"I've something for you, Colleen. It's—well—it isn't

41

fancy—or elegant. I even used it—just a little bit. But I thought it might help.''

She placed a small sketchbook into my hands. I turned it in my hands, sensing the love and importance behind the gift. Then I opened my arms and she stepped into them.

"Thank you," I whispered, swallowing hard. "I promise that the very first sketch you like will belong to you."

"Oh, good!" she cried happily as she darted off.

When I put on my fleece-lined jacket, I slipped the book close to my heart. Then I said good night to Jack and Sherry and headed for my new home at Miss Standby's. Tomorrow I would try again to put my thoughts into pictures.

Before I went to bed, I opened the book. A baby seal with round bright eyes peered at me. I turned the page to see pink clouds and barefoot prints.

Tears pricked my eyes. It was a long time before I finally slept.

I crouched alone on the rocks, Tiffany's sketchbook clutched in my numbed fingers. It was no use. The tumbled rocks, the waves splintering at my feet, the scudding gray clouds all should have been ready subjects for my pencil, but were not.

There had been no sun all morning. The rough, steady tide of late morning, driven by a hard, high wind, brimmed into the rocky pools, churning them into a lather of impatient water. Gulls were blown sideways on the wild air, careening above the roaring waves.

It would be a good hour's hike to return to the more familiar, sandy beaches stretching before Miss Lavender's windows. I turned southward.

A darkened recess on the cliff's rocky face caught my eye. I ignored the rock points beneath me, rising from the quarrelsome restless green water, and climbed upwards, scrambling over rocks and boulders, detouring around others.

Halfway up the cliff's face, I stopped, then bent low

beneath an overhanging rock ledge. My delighted cry was lost in the noise of the surf.

I cautiously stepped inside and found myself standing in a roofed cave floored with fine gray sand. Now the noise of waves, the cry of the gulls and the wind's rough voice were muted.

Reaching up, I pulled off the navy handkerchief tied around my head. My hair fell forward, a mass of wind-blown gold. I shook it back from my face, running my fingers through to smooth it, then dropped cross-legged on the sandy floor.

Bracing my back against the rock's shoulder, I stared out to sea. The moving water and flying spray seemed to belong to another world. I closed my eyes, letting tensed muscles relax.

A phrase from the Psalms leaped into my mind. *The cleft of the rocks,* David said. A hymn from my childhood whispered inside me. *Rock of ages cleft for me, Let me hide myself in Thee* . . .

After a while I resumed my journey south. But I planned to return. Perhaps someday I would bring another person to my cleft in the rock. But that would be when I understood more of what the Lord was trying to teach me. For now it was my own hiding place.

Later I tried to explain to Miss Lavender as I sat in the kitchen eating a grilled cheese sandwich and hot tomato soup. "I couldn't draw," I said, "but I did find a place that said 'special' to me. It was a cave—a cleft in the rock."

A smile stirred in her gray eyes. "Like the hymn?"

I nodded. "I wish I could capture what I felt and put it into neat tidy words. Or better yet, paint it. And I was sorry I couldn't catch something in my sketchbook that would please Tiffany."

"Perhaps you need to try something different."

I swallowed a bite of the sandwich and looked at her intently. "What do you mean?"

"I don't mean something totally different, like sewing or piecing a quilt. I mean a change of scene, a new perspective. Something you've not tried before.''

Thoughtfully, I examined the dips and curls in the antique cherry buffet, then moved to the delicate rose-petaled dishes inside.

My thoughts turned to the outdoors. I remembered the chrysanthemums in the overgrown garden room—the old sundial, then the hill, the woods.''You may be right,'' I said. ''Maybe I need to leave the beach behind for a little while—go to the woods.''

Miss Lavender agreed. ''Yes,'' she said. ''There are mosses there, ferns, exposed roots, many things you might enjoy sketching.''

That afternoon I followed her suggestion. The troubled sky was heavy, the fallen leaves silent and sullen, where only a few days earlier they had laughed and chuckled.

''It will be a miracle if I find anything worth sketching,'' I muttered as I cut across the garden. Several late roses bloomed disconsolately from neglected bushes in what appeared to be the remnant of a sunken garden.

The birch tree lowered its branches protectively around the old sundial. I caught my breath, marveling at the golden leaves still clinging close. A stray breeze stole past my head, moving the leaves, whispering secrets. Even the sundial acquired a personality of aloofness, hinting of an unseen past.

I squatted down, bracing my knees against a large rock, and opened my sketchbook. But the leaves that grew on the page refused to whisper. The sundial stubbornly refused to reveal its quaint old-fashioned charm. What should have been ready art was not.

I snapped the book shut and strode stoically past the murmuring tree. ''Lord . . .'' I whispered as I began ascending the hill. But I was afraid to turn my wish into a prayer.

It was a while before my thoughts stopped turning inward and I began noticing my surroundings: the intricate design in the mosses draped over the vine maple limbs, the delicate perfection of the tiny cones decorating the boughs of the dark green cedars.

The sea had always haunted me. This afternoon it was different. A sense of peace gradually enveloped my spirit.

Memories of childhood rambles in the woods, the exquisite thrill of discovering a tiny mushroom, a circle of moss, then peopling it with tiny imaginary elves in green and brown leaf suits.

I slid my sketchbook out and crouched low over a mushroom nestled among the brown, rotting leaves.

My pencil seemed to move of its own volition. A tiny elf danced with outspread arms upon my mushroom. Another, beneath the slanting roof, tilted his head, peering upward, a look of startled concern on his face.

The rotten stump behind them was transformed into a fantasy castle with windows and sagging turrets and another elf half hidden in the doorway.

Dusk fell and I could no longer see.

My legs felt numb and cold but I didn't care. I smiled. I knew I'd caught something: a blend of fantasy and reality that satisfied.

I hugged my sketchbook close and turned toward home, anticipation warming me. I couldn't wait to share my sketch with Miss Lavender and Tiffany. I ran.

A dark shape stood at the gate. I gasped and skidded to a stop, my heart dipping to my stomach. Consternation filled me as I recognized Alan Nichols—my stranger from the sea.

Regret and sharp chagrin stabbed me. I walked toward him slowly.

"Colleen."

"How did you know my name?"

He smiled and quite suddenly I knew I missed his beard. His chin had a gentle look that was somehow disarming.

He leaned forward, unlatching the gate. "What's that you're hugging?"

I should have been offended, but I wasn't. I stepped inside the yard and smiled. "It's my sketchbook," I explained. "I've been out on the hill entertaining fantasy and fairy tales and—"

Embarrassed, I stopped abruptly. Alan didn't seem to

notice my discomfort. Interest shone from his eyes. Even in the dusk I saw it.

The intentness of his gaze flustered me. "There's—I—shall we go inside?"

At the steps I turned to him. "You haven't told me how you discovered my name."

He laughed easily. "I described you to Jack and Sherry. They knew who you were right away."

A flush rose to my cheeks. *Sherry probably told him everything,* I thought. *Well, I'm just not going to let it matter."*

I lifted my chin courageously. "I want to apologize—I mean—I'm sorry about the way I acted the day of the storm. I didn't even think to say thank you for bringing me to safety."

Alan shook his head. "Don't," he said. "When things crash in around us, we're inclined to forget the ordinary civilities. The night of the banquet—"

"I was rude!" I exclaimed. "But I didn't recognize you."

Alan smiled. "I recognized you right away. In that ivory dress you were a far cry from the bedraggled gull blown in from the sea, but I knew you."

I'd have known you, too, if you hadn't shaved off your beard. He seemed to sense my thoughts, for his hand came up and rubbed his chin.

Quickly I diverted the conversation into other channels. "I prayed for you that night. Were you safe? Where did you go?"

A weary faraway look suddenly veiled his hazel eyes. I changed the subject again. "I live with a lady named Miss Standby—except I call her Miss Lavender. I'd like you to meet her. She's lovely."

Even as I opened the door, she came toward us from the kitchen, a soft pink apron covering a lavender flower-sprigged dress.

"Colleen!" she exclaimed. "You've done it, haven't

you?'' She caught sight of Alan behind me. "Oh, good evening."

"This is Alan Nichols," I said, "the youth pastor at church. Alan, this is Miss Lavender."

He went to her at once, clasping her slender, fragile hand in his. "Miss Lavender. I'd like to call you that, too, if you don't mind. It suits you."

A soft flush rose in her pale cheeks. I was aware of how youthful, how radiant she looked. "Of course you may. Colleen invented it for me and I love it." She turned to me. "Tell me, Marigold, what did you discover?"

Almost shyly I opened my sketchbook. Doubts pricked me. Would my simple forest fantasy stand up under bright lights and the intense scrutiny of others' eyes?

"Why, Colleen," she cried, "they're adorable!"

I lifted my eyes from my pirouetting elves and looked at Alan. For a moment I wished I'd waited to open my book. These strange new creations were too new, too fragile for a stranger's gaze. Would he laugh or criticize? I felt I couldn't bear it if he did.

He did neither. He touched the mushroom gently, and I noticed his long fingers and wide hand—a hand that revealed strength and vitality.

He turned to me with wonder in his eyes. "You've caught something beautiful. I wonder how you did it."

6 / The Mouse

Miss Lavender reached out and turned the page. Before us stood my fantasy castle with half-hidden elves, tender mosses tucked inside crevasses, lichens, a curling maple leaf before the door . . .

"I'm going to add some color," I said. "Greens, grays, a muted gold on that fallen leaf."

"Pink clouds perhaps," Alan murmured. "With a woodland pool reflecting—"

"Make it a morning picture," Miss Lavender interrupted eagerly, "with a little girl elf combing her hair and looking at herself in the water." She touched the elf in the doorway. "See, he's peeking."

I stared at the sketch, remembering a pink sunrise, running figures racing toward the sea . . . I looked up. Alan's eyes met mine. *What happened to my painting?* I wanted to ask. *Was it you that day who walked away?*

Something I didn't understand sealed my lips. I closed my sketchbook abruptly and turned to Miss Lavender. "It was your suggestion that did it. Thank you."

Miss Lavender smiled. *It's her silver smile,* I noted. I had a desire to call it to Alan's attention, but I didn't.

Instead I said, "I'm going to brew a pot of tea. Would you both join me?"

We all trooped into Miss Lavender's kitchen. I put the teakettle on the stove and rummaged in the cupboard. "Cinnamon, Orange-Almond, English Breakfast?"

I brewed it carefully, Miss Lavender's watchful eye on me as I warmed the teapot and measured the tea. The heartening almond scented the room as I poured the amber liquid.

Miss Lavender took a slow, careful sip. "You did it just right, Colleen. It's perfect."

I laughed. "With you as a teacher, how could I fail?" I poured myself a cup and joined them at the table.

We had a good time getting to know each other. The tea flowed and so did our talk. I could tell Alan was fascinated by Miss Lavender. He kept turning to her, drawing her into the conversation.

I felt a tinge of regret when he pushed back his chair and stood up. "I have to go," he said.

"You'll come again?" Miss Lavender asked.

Alan's gaze caught mine. A flush rose into my cheeks. "Please do," I said.

As he went out the door, expectancy stirred in me. Why this sense of mystery I seemed to feel in his presence? Was it because he'd rescued me from the storm, then disappeared? Because I hadn't recognized him at the dinner?

Maybe it's the painting, I mused. *I'm almost sure I saw him that day with something beneath his arm.*

That evening Pete called. "I have Thanksgiving weekend off," he said gaily. "I'll be at the beach house, cleaning and evaluating. Can we spend Thanksgiving together?"

A curious flatness invaded my voice. "Why, Pete," I said slowly, "I guess so. I'll have to ask Miss Lavender—"

"I wasn't inviting myself to dinner," Pete protested. "I wanted to take you out. There's a really neat restaurant in Newport. We could drive." His voice lowered. "It would be nice, just the two of us."

"But I can't, Pete! Miss Lavender's looking forward to our being together. She's all alone. We're planning Cornish hens and pumpkin pie . . . Pete, are you there?"

"Yes, of course. I was just thinking. Are you sure we couldn't work something out? Perhaps the minister and his wife could have her over."

"I'll try to figure something, Pete. I'll—" I caught a glimpse of Miss Lavender out of the corner of my eye. "I'll call you back."

Miss Lavender moved into my line of vision. She'd changed into an orchid and silver robe that enhanced her fragile beauty. Vaguely I wondered why she'd never married. Someday, perhaps, I'd ask her.

"I couldn't help hearing those last words," Miss Lavender said. "Was it your young man?"

"Mine?" I spluttered. Alan leaped into my thoughts. Ruthlessly I shoved him aside. "It was Pete," I explained. "You haven't met him."

I sat down on the couch and leaned forward. "In a way he is my young man—I guess. He's played an important part in my life."

Elbows on my knees, I rested my chin in my hands, one finger tracing my eyebrow.

"Pete came into my life when I needed someone with stability. Maybe Christlikeness would be a better word." I hesitated, searching for words to describe the girl who had raced headlong away from responsibility, family, and God.

"Go on," Miss Lavender encouraged.

"I wanted something I couldn't seem to find." My voice lowered. "I still haven't . . . Anyway, Pete came into my life. He never told me I *had* to do anything. He was just there, encouraging me. Sometimes we'd talk about Christ, who He is, how He fit into our lives."

I spread my hands wide. "At that time Jesus Christ was practically nil—I mean as far as fitting into my life."

"Is it different now?" Miss Lavender asked.

"Yes. When Pete suggested I live in his house while he was away, it made a difference. I began to think. Things began to change. Except lately Pete's been different, sort of hovering, overprotective. And all of a sudden he's got this idea I should go to art school."

"That might not be a bad idea."

"I know. It's just that he seems to want to mold me, push me out as a socialite or something." I laced my fingers together and leaned forward earnestly. "That's not me, Miss Lavender. At least I don't think it is."

"Then what is you?" Miss Lavender asked, her steady gray eyes searching mine. "What do you really want?"

"Just to paint. But even more important—" I took a deep breath. "There's a little spot deep inside me that yearns for God. I don't know why I keep running—pushing Him away.''

"Your fear of responsibility? Commitment?"

"I think it's more than that. Alan would probably say I had a rebellious heart.''

"Alan? How did he get into this?"

A flush rose into my cheeks. "He's a preacher, isn't he? Don't they always?'' I stood up abruptly. "You need a cat, Miss Lavender. I'm surprised you don't have one,'' I said, changing the subject.

Miss Lavender refused to be sidetracked. "This Pete,'' she pursued, "where's he from?''

"I met him back home. His folks live there. He's in the Coast Guard now, stationed at Garibaldi.''

"You should ask him to spend Thanksgiving with us,'' she said graciously. "It's hard to be far from home on such a family day.''

I opened my mouth to object, then shut it firmly.

"Thank you, Miss Lavender. I'll tell him he's welcome.''

That night I lay staring into the darkness, wondering why I wasn't anticipating spending the holiday with Pete. I sketched his profile in my mind: full lips, firm forehead, classic nose.

Sleep came and with it a dream. Pete and I stood on a tall bluff overlooking the ocean. Waves sparkled in the sunshine.

Even as I looked I saw wind patterns tracing little paths across the water. "Known unto Him are the paths of the sea,'' Pete said in my dream.

I wakened quickly, the little silver paths sharp in my consciousness. Moonlight flooded the room. My dresser stood out sharply, the mirror above it glinting back silver light. A soft breeze moved the ruffled priscillas at the window, whispering an invitation.

I sat up, then crept to the window. My breath caught in pure wonder. Silver moonlight rested on the roofs of the sleeping houses. The laurel leaves, forbidding and depressing by day, were transformed into shimmering paths.

If only I could capture them in a painting. Silver paths crossing and recrossing with that elusive sense of distance— mystery. Known unto God are the paths of the sea . . .

A pattering sound, almost like a faucet discharging its contents in quick, successive drops, interrupted my thoughts. The swift, little dashes came again.

"Mice!" I exclaimed. I dropped the curtain and leapt for the bed, furrowing deep inside my blanket. The house, silent once more, brooded around me.

Then the pitter-patter came again. This time my imagination came to my rescue, turning the sound into a soft clack-clack, like the chattering of tiny teeth shuddering from cold—my woodland elves escaping from the elements, seeking haven inside the warm walls.

My comforting illusion vanished, however, as a gnawing began. I bolted upright and reached for a shoe beside the bed. As I thumped it against the wall, the noise stopped.

I smiled and lay back down. Sleep had begun to whisper at the edges of consciousness when the noise began again.

"Nibble, nibble." Silence. Then, "Gnaw, gnaw, gnaw."

"Silence!" I yelled, then clapped my hand over my mouth at my thoughtlessness. Fortunately Miss Lavender's hearing wasn't too keen. The mouse stopped, then started again.

I reached for my shoe. Again I whacked the wall—more softly this time. Again there was silence.

I lay back down, turning onto my side, trying to recapture my dream—*silver ocean paths (moonlit laurel ones)— Pete—my house on the beach—*

"Gnaw, gnaw." That mouse was making fun of me! I shot out of bed and flipped on the light switch.

Silence. But I wasn't fooled. He was inside my walls, chewing and grinding, thinking he was safe and secure. I'd show him!

I opened the closet and took out a wire hanger with which I could hopefully jab into the wall through any chance opening. As I untwisted the hanger, my eyes searched the clothes closet. I leaned forward and shoved the clothes aside.

"Those builders knew how to make sturdy houses," I muttered, "but I know I saw a crack somewhere."

I backed out, feeling slightly suffocated, and examined my surroundings. Waist-high wainscoting circled the room. Perhaps I could pry open a loosened board.

I prowled around the room, brandishing my bent clothes hanger in one hand, pushing and shoving against each board with the other. My only reward was a broken fingernail.

"Well," I said gloomily, "there are such things as traps and mouse poison."

Cold and weariness were catching up with me. I sighed, wondering if my noisy fumbling had frightened the mouse away. Probably not.

Before I lay down my wire weapon and flipped the light switch, I read the golden words on the sampler over my bed: "The path of the just is as a shining light."

It reminded me of my dream and the silver paths on the sea.

I turned off the light and slipped into bed. If only my mouse would stay away and let sleep claim me.

Almost at once the gnawing began again. I sat up, drawing my knees to my chest, my eyes probing the moonlit shadowed room.

"You win, Mr. Mouse. It's the couch in the living room for me." I got up and draped myself with a blanket, Indian style.

The gnawing continued. My mouse was getting bolder. He knew I was helpless.

I wandered to the window for one last look at the moon-drenched countryside. As I leaned against the window, the sill moved beneath my hands.

"Just one minute, Mouse. I'm going to get inside your domain after all."

I pushed up on the edge of the board. It tipped. Elation filled me as I lifted the sill.

The gnawing stopped abruptly. Impulsively I plunged my hands into the opening. Instead of emptiness my questing fingers touched an oblong object—a small black book.

I drew it out and turned the book in my hands, then opened it. The moonlight shimmered against silver old-fashioned script:

My Diary—Summer, 1922.

7 / The Black Diary

Summer, 1922. I flipped on the light and opened the diary. Spidery handwriting from the past covered the page. Eagerly my eyes sought for a clue to the writer's identity.

"It could have belonged to Miss Lavender," I mused, "but wait—" The name Lawrence Redgate filled the page, written again and again in meticulous fashion.

I sat down on the edge of the bed. "This is a girl's diary—it has to be."

Already I knew something about her. *Lawrence Redgate is the man she loves. She can't express her feelings except by writing his name over and over again.*

I turned the page impatiently. Could it have belonged to Miss Lavender? Had she once been in love? And if she had been, why had she never married?

The old-fashioned script began stiffly, awkwardly. I had to concentrate to decipher it.

My name is Amelia Standby. I live with my parents and my sister, Opal, at the end of Poplar Street in a little house with a gabled roof.

"That's here," I whispered. "These words could have been written right here in this room." A sense of long ago came over me.

I'm writing this because I have to tell someone—anyone—about the summer I followed the moonpath.

The writing warmed, began to come alive. *It all began the day Lawrence Redgate came to visit my father. He stood by the fireplace and I watched the light gleam off his dark hair.*

"Why, this is a love story," I whispered. I read on.

My sister came in and I felt suddenly angry—he was so

handsome—so debonair. I knew that if she were there, he'd not look at me.

Oh, I know we teasingly called her Miss Wallflower. But she wasn't anything like that. Wherever she went the boys flocked around her—like bees heading straight to the honey.

"Miss Wallflower must be Opal—Miss Lavender."

My thoughts whirled. Lawrence Redgate. Who was he? How did he fit into Miss Lavender's life? Why had she never mentioned her sister, Amelia? She'd only told me she was all alone with no family other than church family.

Anyway, Lawrence stood there. And right away I wanted him to notice me, not Opal. She didn't see me at all as I stood outside the kitchen door. Then it happened, just like I dreamed it would. He looked right past her and saw me, and he smiled. I knew at that moment I'd be drawn to him.

But I never dreamed it would be something that would eventually drive us apart.

"Miss Lavender should be reading this, not me." I leapt to my feet, shutting the black diary with a bang. Before I could change my mind, I stuffed it back inside the windowsill. In the morning I would talk to her.

I lingered at the window, brushing the white ruffles aside and staring into the night. The shadowy hedge heightened the inky darkness. As my eyes adjusted, I was able to discern the outlines of trees, a bush's bumpy shape.

The hedge branches quivered. I leaned forward. For a brief moment, a large light shape stood out against the blackness. I shuddered. Could it be the same wild yellow dog which had attacked me?

I peered intently as it took several halting, uncertain steps, then stumbled forward. Compassion moved inside me. The dog must be sick or injured.

Even as I wondered, the creature disappeared into the shadows. I waited in vain for it to reappear, then went back to bed. I'd check it out in the safety of daylight.

Sleep eluded me. The mouse stayed quiet, but my thoughts were somersaulting into the past. I pictured the man leaning against the fireplace mantle.

I must have dozed for a moment because suddenly in my dream I was there. The man turned toward me, and my knees turned to water. He winked and I recognized Alan Nichols. Startled, I awakened.

The mouse was gnawing again beneath the windowsill. Could he be chewing up Amelia's little black treasury of memories and dreams?

Once again I hopped out of bed. I put the diary under my pillow and reached for my sketchbook.

A face grew beneath my fingers. This was supposed to be a man I'd never met, leaning against the fireplace mantle, his eyes alive with interest for a pretty girl, but his beard was shaped like Alan's. Even the gentle hazel eyes smiling at me belonged to Alan.

The mouse resumed his restless gnawing, but this time I only smiled. I turned the page in my sketchbook. "This will be for Tiffany," I murmured.

A cartoonish mouse with teasing eyes swung from a bedpost. Another, his tiny feet planted on a black book, peered around a hole with roughened edges. Still another ran across the keys of an antique organ.

Late November sunshine welcomed me as I stepped into the breakfast nook, my sketchbook in hand. Tea and tiny biscuits covered with strawberry marmalade gladdened my eye.

So did Miss Lavender's silver smile. "Goodness!" she exclaimed. "I thought you were going to sleep the morning away."

"It was because of the mouse," I explained. "He gnawed for hours—but I got rid of him." I put my sketchbook down on the table in front of her with a flourish. "Look, I captured him here—and his dreadful little henchmen."

Miss Lavender leaned forward. "Oh, Colleen, I like him. I can almost hear him gnawing. Did he keep you awake all night?"

"No, not quite. But he did a pretty good job of it. I hope I didn't disturb you when I banged the wall."

Miss Lavender shook her head. "I didn't hear a thing. But then my hearing isn't as keen as it once was." She looked intently at the mouse perched on top of the diary, his tiny feet clinging to the book's edge. "What's that?" she asked. "What is he standing on?"

"A diary," I said. "I started to read it but thought better of it."

"A diary?"

"It was inside the wall, under the windowsill. I found it while I was trying to get at the mouse." I hesitated. "It belonged to Amelia."

Miss Lavender started, her eyes widened.

"My *sister* Amelia? Colleen, you must be mistaken! My sister has been dead over fifty years!"

I saw consternation and disbelief in her silver gray eyes. "I probably shouldn't have read it," I said, "but I'm not mistaken. She wrote, 'My name is Amelia Standby and I'm writing to tell about the summer of 1922'—or something like that."

Miss Lavender stood up abruptly. I noticed her hands, the quick awkward movements so unlike her usual smooth, gentle gestures.

"It's a love story," I said.

"1922," she whispered. "It could be—it just might be . . . ."

"It is," I insisted. "The writing is old-fashioned, kind of spidery. But," I hastened to explain, "I only read a little bit—just enough to discover her name."

"A voice from the past." Her voice caught. "I'd like to see it, Colleen."

I put down the butter knife and stood. "After Mr. Mouse started gnawing again, I decided the windowsill wasn't the safest place. It's under my pillow now."

I hurried up the stairs, pulling the diary out from beneath the snowy pillow, fingering the black edges. I frowned. Miss Lavender's discomfort bothered me.

I addressed the book uneasily. "You'd better have good things to say to Miss Lavender. She's a dear." I opened the diary to the front page and traced the lettering, my lower lip caught between my teeth.

"It's funny. She did act strange just now. I wonder what secrets are held inside this little black book."

My wonderings would have to wait. I stifled my desire to open the pages and continue the story I'd begun in the night. As I went down the stairs, I wondered if she would ever let me read it.

She took the book eagerly, exclaiming, "It looks familiar!" Something flickered in her eyes. Was it fear?

"Open it," I encouraged. "Her name is inside—Amelia Standby."

Miss Lavender's eyes scurried to mine. I saw uncertainty surface in them. "I'm almost afraid. It's been so long."

Impulsively I put my arms around her. "She's your sister," I encouraged. "She loved you."

"Did she? Sometimes I wonder. I was not always kind to her."

I cringed as I remembered Amelia's words. *My sister came in and I felt suddenly angry;* then later, *I never dreamed it would be something that would eventually drive us apart.* But she'd been talking about Lawrence then, hadn't she?

I wished I could go back into time before I'd told Miss Lavender about the diary.

Should I have let well enough alone instead of dragging it into the light of day? Should I have stuffed the diary beneath the windowsill where it wouldn't trouble anyone?

I think Miss Lavender caught a glimpse of my thoughts, for she said, "Don't worry, Colleen. Whatever she wrote here has been written for a half century. It will be good to look back and see her as I remembered her."

"I'll leave you here to read it alone. I'll go to the sea and let the waves talk to me."

Her hug was warm and responsive. "Go, my dear. Enjoy. When you return we'll talk."

I smiled at her as I went for my coat, thankful for the reappearance of her silver look, that poised, queenly bearing

I so much admired. But when I slipped outside several minutes later I wondered. Miss Lavender was always so serene, so much in control. Would she ever be able to share her life, her hurts?

Fog was beginning to blow in from the sea, obliterating the blueness of the morning sky. I walked gratefully into its billowing protection, letting it enclose me.

Its misty fingers touched my cheeks gently. I shivered, then turned. Already the fog had cut off the top of the hill that I'd peopled with imaginary elves. The trees were entwined with feathery wisps. I reached up and touched the edge of the sketchbook I'd tucked beneath my coat. Perhaps . . .

But the sea beckoned with a mighty persuasive roar. I turned away from the hills and ran toward the beach.

White chargers thundered to meet me, their heads thrown back, their mane and tails flying. I stopped. The fog swirled around me, enclosing me in its cool softness. I was in a world alone, protected—wrapped in a cocoon . . .

A man's figure emerged from the mist, jogging where the waves met the sand. My heart plunged treacherously. Alan.

Even as I watched, he moved to chase a wave, then turned inland and away—away. He shifted again, running toward me.

I saw surprise and a kind of gladness sparkle in his face. "Colleen!" he called, "come run with me!"

A shaft of wind blew the fog apart. For a brief moment sunshine shone against the sand. My spirit tingled in response to the sun, to his call. I turned and ran ahead of him.

Alan caught up with me and we ran shoulder to shoulder. "Isn't it glorious!" I cried, with a gesture that included the waves, the sand, the very air around us.

"Yes!" he shouted. "Nothing grander than running on the beach!"

"Except spinning down a hydrotube!"

"That too!" He reached up and wiped his forehead,

grinning broadly. "Maybe we'll do that together someday."

I didn't answer, but once again I felt that plunge inside me. We ran without words for several minutes. My breath began coming in ragged gasps, my side to ache. I slowed to a walk. "I'm not used to this!" I gasped.

"Me either," Alan agreed. He reached over and grabbed my hand, then gestured to a piece of driftwood ahead of us, rearing into the air. It reminded me of a dinosaur, a relic from the past.

"It's Dino," I said. "See its jaw, the armor on its neck."

Again I saw surprised wonder glint in his hazel eyes. *He looked that way when I showed him my elves.*

"It's my artist's eye," I explained self-consciously. "No—not totally. I think it's a way of seeing things that I inherited from my grandad. He saw designs in stump rings, animals in the shapes of trees."

Alan released my hand and I dropped to my knees in the sand mounded around Dino's stomach. I braced my back against his sturdy thigh and turned to face Alan.

His face was reddened from the wind and our brisk run. Almost without realizing it, my mind began to sketch the hair springing in soft waviness away from his forehead, the eyebrows with the rebellious hairs turning backward—

"What are you thinking when your eyes cloud up with those sea colors?" he asked, interrupting my thoughts. "They go faraway, even though you're looking at me."

My cheeks flushed. "I don't mean to stare or move away," I apologized. "Sometimes I just get the urge to capture something in my sketchbook. Those hairs in your eyebrows—several of them grow in the wrong direction."

Alan threw back his head and laughed hilariously. I felt the red in my face deepen, matching the red in the T-shirt beneath my coat.

"I don't know what's so funny," I said haughtily. Feeling warm and uncomfortable, I unzipped my coat and tossed it onto the sand.

Alan sobered immediately. "It's just that you say things

most girls don't even think about—or if they do think them—"

"But I didn't mean it badly! About the hairs in your eyebrows, they just have a way of personalizing you."

"I know that, Colleen." He touched my hand. "You're a unique girl."

His hand discomfitted me. Gently I slid mine away and began digging in the wet sand. "I like it when its moldable," I said. "When it's dry it doesn't hold shape—sifts through my fingertips—"

"And sucks up water like a giant sponge, pops dimples from flea burrows," he finished.

"It does do that, doesn't it?" I said eagerly. "Have you noticed the sea when the tide goes out—the way it sucks dry the great tide-splashed sand lakes?"

Alan looked at me intently. "You really love the ocean, don't you?"

"Yes," I confessed. "It's a part of me somehow. Whenever I'm discouraged or troubled, it's the first place I go."

Alan rocked back on his heels. "Is that why you came this morning?"

His question brought the black diary and Miss Lavender's agitation into my thoughts. I stopped digging my sand mountain. "I suppose so."

"Is it something you can tell me? Something you'd feel free to share?"

"It's about Miss Lavender," I said slowly. "She—she—" I raised troubled eyes to his. "Last night I found something from her past. It was a diary hidden inside my wall."

I laughed ruefully. "I was mouse hunting. Anyway, to make a long story short, I discovered it, and even read some of it before my conscience got to me. I gave it to her this morning. She seemed disturbed. I know she was."

"Because you read it?"

"Partly. And partly because I think things between her sister and her weren't all they could have been. She seemed so unlike her usual calm self."

"Angry?"

"No, not really. Upset, though. Her sister died, you know, apparently right after she'd written the diary. I wonder . . . Could there be thoughts inside that will hurt Miss Lavender? She's such a lovely lady—"

"You had to give it to her, Colleen. After all, it *did* belong to her sister. How would you feel if your sister died and afterward you found her diary? Wouldn't you want to read it?"

"Melissa! Of course. But Melissa would never have anything in it that would hurt me!"

"But even if she did, you'd want to know her thoughts, wouldn't you?"

My thoughts plunged into my own past. When I'd run away from home, Melissa had read my diary. I remembered how some secret part of me wanted her to find it—read it—so she might somehow understand what was happening deep inside me.

"I think I would," I said. "People who are close to you are awfully important. I'm beginning to see that now."

"Families are exceedingly important."

I thought I saw hurt stir and a sudden memory veil his eyes. I had an immediate longing to reach up and smooth those rebellious hairs.

Instead I asked, "Do you have one? A family I mean?"

"Yes—and no. My real mother died when I was little." He leapt to his feet, spattering sand across my coat.

He didn't seem to notice. His eyes were on the charging waves.

He turned to me. "Don't worry about Miss Lavender and the diary, Colleen. Let God take care of her." He gestured oceanward. "He's powerful—big enough to handle any crisis."

I stood up, brushed sand off my blue jeans, grabbed my coat and tied its arms around my waist.

We took off together, side by side. The wind, the sky and a tiny piece from the past ran with us.

8 / Follow the Moonpath

"I love the beach!" I cried. The wind pushed against me, lifting my hair off my shoulders. The damp sand was smooth beneath our feet.

A sandpiper tripped comically along where white-fringed waves curled to reach him. He hopped in a quick dance step as a wave swept in. As we came closer he raced headlong across the sand, his diminutive tail bobbing like a cork on a troubled pond.

I started to laugh; I couldn't help myself. Alan snorted in amusement. Our sandpiper didn't join us. He spread his wings and lifted himself into the air. "He didn't think much of our laughter," I gasped. "See, he's even flying indignantly!"

It was true. His wings flopped up and down in graceful scorn. We watched him wing his way high into the sky, becoming a faint dot.

"Think you could make it to your house on the beach?" Alan asked.

"I'm not sure. If we stopped sometimes."

We slowed to a walk. I took a deep breath and grinned at him. "Do you run a lot on the beach?"

"If I get the chance, you bet."

"That night—I mean the afternoon of the storm—did you come back here?"

I watched his face, saw his brows pull together. "No, Colleen. Why do you ask?"

"I prayed for you that night. I wondered if you were all right. And," I persisted, "I thought I saw you the next day at my house."

Alan's brisk pace slowed. He stopped and flashed a piercing look at me. I felt my cheeks redden. "You don't have to tell me," I said. "I just wondered."

"It's all right."

But I sensed hesitancy in his voice. I started walking ahead of him, embarrassed at my obvious feeling. He apparently didn't need—or want—my concern. He caught up with me and grabbed my arm. I lifted my chin haughtily and tried not to look at him. But he ignored my cold withdrawal.

"Colleen," he protested, "you don't understand."

"I don't have to understand," I said brusquely. "I'm not your keeper, and what you do is certainly none of my business."

How could I explain how I'd felt that night, the sense of urgency that had compelled me to pray? Especially when I couldn't even understand it myself?

I veered away from my feelings, afraid of my own vulnerability. "I saw an animal come out of the hedge last night. It looked sick—or hurt. I was going to check it out this morning, but I forgot."

Alan jerked to a stop. "Could it be the dog Jack told me about? The one that attacked you?"

I turned around. "Probably. But I don't know." I looked at his face and saw the concern reflected in the depths of his eyes. *What is there about this man that touches my heart?* I wondered.

Impulsively I stretched out my hand to him. "Come on," I said, "don't look so worried. I'll be quite okay."

I took several little running steps backward, then veered on my heel. We were off again, the waves beside us, the sun and clouds making shadows on the sand, the wet expanse disturbed only by a few clumps of brown sea kelp. Little swirls of fog dipped like transient ghostlings, bobbing, dancing, dropping a curtsy here and there. Mostly we ran without words, sometimes slowing to a brisk walk, once stopping for a short rest on a sand-embedded log.

The house I'd spent so many contented hours in with my painting was as I remembered it, except the windows facing the sea were blank, the roof gone.

I slowed to a walk but Alan kept running. At the door,

he turned and shouted, "Someone's been here! Everything's gone!"

Something cold dipped into the pit of my stomach. "Pete. I hope it was Pete."

I hurried forward. The floor, though wet, was swept clean of debris and broken glass. Desolation swept through me.

"It's an abandoned home," I said quietly, "not like my little house of dreams."

"Where is everything?"

"Pete took it. But I didn't know he'd cleaned everything out. He said last night he was going to do it Thanksgiving weekend."

"He must have changed his mind."

A car roared close to the house. I ran to the window. A tall young man opened the car door and strode toward the house. "It's Pete now!"

I ran to the door. "Why, Colleen," Pete cried, "this is a surprise!"

His long arms wrapped me in a warm bear hug, lifting me off the floor. "Pete," I laughed, trying desperately to disengage myself, "I'd like you to meet Alan."

Pete's arms dropped to his sides.

Alan stepped forward, his hand held out. "I'm Alan Nichols," he said, "and you're Pete?"

Pete looked at him warily. I was sure I saw dislike gathering in his blue eyes. His hand came out slowly. "Yes, I'm Pete—Pete Erickson." He looked at me intently, questions clouding his gaze.

"Alan is the new youth pastor in our church," I explained. "He spoke at the harvest dinner and—"

"I'm relatively new in the area," Alan interjected. "Colleen has been showing me around." He gestured toward the house. "I'm sorry about what happened."

Pete shrugged. "It's the breaks," he said philosophically. "Already I'm planning to rebuild. I'll be spending my time off sawing and hammering."

"If you're here on the weekends, come to church," Alan

invited. "We'd be glad to see you." He turned to me. "Shall we head back?"

"Back?" Pete questioned. "Do you mean you walked all the way from town?"

"Ran would be a better word," I said tartly. "It was fun, though."

Pete's eyes swept over me. "You shouldn't have," he said. "That's too far—"

"Not really," I protested.

The two men's eyes met. *Like two cats meeting—neither one quite trusting.* I had a strong desire to get the two away from one another. But how?

Pete and Alan solved my dilemma with a few words, "I'm going back to town to pick up supplies," Pete said. "You two can ride along."

Alan shook his head. "I'm not ready to return," he said. "But Colleen might like a lift."

Quite suddenly I didn't want to go home. Pete's hand tugging on mine irritated me. I shrugged it off abruptly. "Not now!" I said.

Pete's handsome brows shot upwards. "But, Colleen . . ."

"All right, I'll come," I said ungraciously. Shame at my behavior softened my tone, "I'm sorry." I smiled at him apologetically, then glanced at Alan out of the corner of my eye. Already he was walking toward the door. He turned.

"It was good meeting you, Pete. Colleen, I'll see you in town, maybe in church." He inclined his head. "The run was glorious. Thanks for your time."

Then he was gone. I stared after him, a lonely figure walking on the beach, his head slightly lowered. Then he was running, his stride eating up the distance.

"So he's a preacher man," Pete said softly. "It seems he's more than that—at least to you."

I whirled to face him. "You have no right to say that!" I snapped.

Pete ignored my anger. "So you met him at church,"

he mused. "What did he do, pick you out of the bevy?"

It wasn't that way, my thoughts cried. *But even if it had been, I'd not tell you!*

"Colleen, I'm sorry," Pete said, suddenly contrite. "I shouldn't have said that."

"You should have been with us on the beach, Pete," I said, still angry but trying to calm myself. "The fog was beautiful, swirling in bits and pieces."

"I'm sorry, Colleen," Pete repeated, "I shouldn't have—"

"No, you shouldn't have, but you did. Come on, let's go. I need a cup of tea or maybe a sandwich."

"I'll take you to the Oyster Shoppe," Pete said. "We'll have lunch and talk."

But irritation chafed my spirits, so as I got into the car I said, "I'd rather not, Pete. Miss Lavender is expecting me."

Pete backed out of the driveway, his head turned to one side. "Like fun," he grumbled. "You *were* going to walk those three miles."

He was right, but I wasn't going to admit it. I chose to ignore his words. "I'd rather go home," I said stiffly.

The steering wheel whirled beneath Pete's hands. "As you please."

I sucked in my breath and stared stonily out the window. Pete's hand stole over mine.

The silence between us grew as we drove back to town. Pete slowed at the church and stared at it, his thoughts caught away.

"Jack Mitchell's a neat teacher," I volunteered, "and I really like the people, now that I'm getting to know them."

"Maybe I'll come sometime when I have a Sunday off," he said slowly. "Yes, I think I will."

As we turned into Miss Lavender's, his eyes met mine. "I've been a real boor, Colleen. I hope that doesn't mean we can't still be friends."

"It's all right," I said. "I guess I haven't been too friendly myself. But, Pete, just because you helped me over a rough spot doesn't mean you *own* me—"

"Of course I don't," Pete interrupted. "It's just that you're so special. I hate it when I see other guys looking at you like that."

"Like what!" I spluttered, irritation rising again.

"The way that Alan did. He likes you."

"Oh, Pete, he does not! I'm just someone he's trying to help!" My voice lowered. "Like you did."

Pete's hands rubbed the steering wheel. "That's what you think, girl. That's what you think."

I thought about his words as I let myself into the living room. Was it true that both Alan and Pete were attracted to me?

My thoughts were forgotten when I saw Miss Lavender. She stood inside the kitchen doorway, her face white, her lips trembling. I sprang to her side.

"Miss Lavender! What is it? What's wrong?"

"I hurt her," she whispered. "I didn't mean to, but I did."

"Miss Lavender!" I cried. I hugged her close, feeling the quiver of her body.

"Was it the diary? Oh, I'm sorry—so sorry!"

"I'm all right, Colleen," she said as she drew a choking breath.

I moved back, my hands still holding her frail shoulders. "You're as white as a sheet. You'd better sit down." Gently I drew her to the couch. She sank into its gray softness, and I sat beside her, holding her hand tightly and willing my strength to reach out to her, to hold her up. A whisper from Alan's words brushed the edges of my thoughts. I grabbed hold of it like a drowning man clutching a raft.

"Trust her to God, Colleen. He's powerful, strong enough for any crisis."

Then another whisper, this one from Melissa's letter. She'd written a verse from Isaiah: "They that wait upon the Lord shall renew their strength; they shall mount up with wings as eagles; they shall run and not be weary; they shall walk and not faint."

Renew our strength, Lord, I prayed. *Quiet our hearts.*

"Tell me," I said aloud, "what's hurting you?"

Her hand tightened on mine. "Amelia's young man," she said falteringly; "he left because of me." Her head bowed.

"Oh, Colleen, it happened long ago. But it's almost as if it were yesterday. I did flirt with him disgracefully. But I never knew—never dreamed it was pulling them apart. She died after he left and I never knew. Oh, yes, I knew something was troubling her, that something had broken our closeness . . . ."

I picked up her clenched hand and rubbed it. "What else did she say?"

Miss Lavender's trembling hand returned to her lap. "Her diary brought it all back. That summer—that turbulent summer—she talked about his going away to the Army and being left alone. She wrote something strange in her diary too." She gestured toward the organ and I saw the small black book tucked in among the Kewpie dolls. "Could you get it for me?"

I rose and placed it in her hand. She clutched it for a moment, then leafed through the pages.

With a quivering voice she began reading. " 'All I have to remember Lawrence with is the silver pendant. But it's a family heirloom and I must return it. I can't do it yet. It's all I have. I'll hide it in a safe place. I'm following the moonpath in the garden—the path we walked hand in hand— before Opal came between us.' "

I looked up. "What does she mean? What pendant? What moonpath?

Miss Lavender shook her head. "I don't know. But those words brought back a memory. She was sick, Colleen, so very sick. Her fingers kept picking at the blanket. She was delirious I thought. Sometimes I'd try to hold her hands and she'd hang on tightly, whispering, 'Follow the moonpath, Opal. Just follow the moonpath. It leads to the sun. . . . ' "

Excitement surged through me. I leapt to my feet. "The sampler in my room!" I cried, "Did it belong to Amelia?"

Miss Lavender's silver brows drew together. Something stirred in her gray eyes. "But of course," she said. "She made that before she got sick—while she was waiting for news of Lawrence."

"Couldn't it mean something?" I demanded. "I mean, it says, 'The path of the just is a shining light . . .' "

" 'That shineth more and more unto the perfect day.' That's the rest of the verse. It's from Proverbs. But I don't understand what you're getting at, Colleen."

"I'm not sure either," I mumbled. "It's just that shining path and moonpath seem connected.

Miss Lavender sighed, then stood. I watched her anxiously but she seemed to have regained control. Whatever her true feelings were, she hid them well.

"I'm going to my room now, Colleen." She gave me a reassuring smile, hesitated a fraction of a moment, then leaned forward and put the diary in my hand.

"I want you to read it for yourself, Colleen. There were things in it for me—but there's something there for you, too." She walked across the room with her regal head held high.

9 / Elusive Paths

The silent room brooded around me. I looked down at the black book in my hand. Did I really want to know its secrets?

To distract myself, I walked over to the Kewpies tucked inside the organ cubbyholes. "Were you here when Lawrence Redgate stood in the doorway and looked at Amelia?" I asked.

Their eternal smiling faces mocked me. I had the impulse to poke my finger into their round pink tummies. Instead, I turned and went up the stairs.

The golden path of Amelia's sampler drew me. I stood and looked at it, my eyes examining the green and gold threads, the intricacies of the stitches. The colors, lustrous and unfaded, seemed untouched by time. I wondered what Amelia had thought as she'd pushed her needle through the cloth, bending close to examine each perfect stitch.

"What secret do *you* hold?" I asked impulsively. I felt the desire to enter the picture and probe the edges of the path for a hidden silver pendant.

"You're growing fanciful," I murmured to myself. "It must be your woodland creatures come to haunt you."

The moonlit path glowed softly. Gently I fingered its smoothness, wondering . . . wondering . . .

A dog barked and I was instantly distracted. The creature I'd seen in the night—the one who'd crawled out of the hedge. Had it been sick?

I hurried to the window and stared down at the hedge. I remembered the blue forget-me-nots that had brightened it earlier. Now there was nothing to relieve its mood. It brooded sullenly, caught away in the darkened corner of its past.

Was the dog who had attacked me lying there—alone?

I put the diary on my bed and scampered down the stairs.

The cold November wind pressed against my face as I let myself out the back door. A billowing thundercloud cut its profile into the sky. I shuddered, then hurried toward the hedge.

Hesitating for a moment, I carefully parted the laurel leaves. The smell of rotting decayed leaves and damp earth smote my nose.

It was awhile before I could make out the tangled undergrowth in the murky darkness. I thrust my head and shoulders deeper into the leaves.

A quick gasp escaped me as I saw a large mounded form lying beneath distant webbed branches inside a slightly recessed area resembling a nest.

Slowly, cautiously, I began to move toward it. As my eyes adjusted to the darkness, I saw two eyes watching me intently.

At that moment something slammed hard against my legs. I screamed and fell forward. At the same time I recognized Tiffany's voice crying, "Colleen! Colleen!"

Branches raked my back, my hair fell free across my shoulders as I struggled to back out. "Colleen! Colleen! Are you all right?"

I fell into the open. "Tiffany! Of course I'm all right. What are you thinking!"

I rocked onto my knees and stared at her. Her brown eyes flashed fear. "I thought that wild dog—I mean—well, I came up and all I saw was your feet and knees sticking out! It looked awful."

One hand reached back to rub my back. "You shouldn't have tackled me, Tiffany. Those branches are sharp." Then I saw the love mingled with her fear and softened my words. "It was good of you to be so worried about me."

"But what were you doing, stuck halfway inside that hedge?" Tiffany demanded. "Dad told me about the dog. I thought—"

I smiled chidingly. "I know what you thought. You thought it had eaten me alive and left my hindparts behind."

The fear evaporated from Tiffany's eyes. "You're horrid, Colleen. Really horrid."

I stood up, brushing the mud from my knees, untangling the leaves caught in my hair. I laughed aloud, my fingers still pulling the debris from my hair.

"You may not believe this, Tiffany, but there's an animal in there." I nodded toward the dark green leaves. "It won't hurt us," I assured her. "But I think it's either sick or starving."

"A dog?"

I nodded. "The one that attacked me, I think. But, Tiffany, it can't hurt us now. It's just lying there alone. I want to try to help."

Empathy dawned in her dark eyes. "How?"

"I don't know. I think—I'm not sure. Maybe some warm milk would help."

"We could put it under here!" Tiffany exclaimed, gesturing at the laurel branches before us. "Then it could come out and eat." Her eyes implored me to agree. "I don't want you to crawl back in there, Colleen. It might bite you."

I didn't answer. Instead, I put my arm around her, drawing her toward the house. "We'll get some milk," I said, "then decide."

Inside the warm kitchen, I opened the refrigerator and brought out a carton of milk. Tiffany set a bowl on the counter. "We'll have to warm it."

I took a small saucepan from the cupboard. "I'm just hoping it'll come out and drink. It was so still."

"Maybe it's dead."

I shook my head. "Its eyes were open. It was looking at me." I didn't try to put into words the appeal I had seen in their depths. I knew that as soon as Tiffany departed, I'd crawl back into that cave-like opening and examine the dog more carefully.

Almost as though reading my mind, Tiffany exclaimed, "It'll come out on its own, Colleen! We'll leave the milk close by."

I didn't argue. I gave the milk in the pan a stir, then

touched the surface gently. "It's warm now."

Tiffany carried the bowl outside, carefully balancing it, her eyes intent on its contents. She smoothed fallen leaves aside, set it down and straightened, pushing her long brown hair behind her shoulders. "There. Now we'll go back in and give the poor thing a chance to come out when we're not looking."

Before I could manage a reply, the thunderhead riding the sky burst and a torrent of rain hit us. "Let's go!" I yelled. "I have some sketches I want you to see."

We raced inside, shook the rain from our hair and sat down at the kitchen table. Tiffany's eyes filled with surprised delight as she viewed my woodland elves. "I love them!" she exulted. "They're darling—much better than any seascapes could ever be—

"I'm sorry, Colleen," she cried, noting my hurt expression. "I've never seen your sea paintings. I really don't know anything about them."

I picked up the sketch of the elf maiden combing her hair. "Don't fret, Tiffany. They were a part of my life—just like these little creatures are. Someday I'll do another seascape. Only my next one will be better."

I lifted my head, images forming in my mind. A moonlit path across a silver sea—tall cliffs jutting into the night sky—a man, a girl—silhouettes against the moon . . .

I suddenly longed for Tiffany to be gone. I wanted to be alone to catch the vision of silver seas and moonlit paths.

Instead I turned the page. "Mice!" Tiffany said. "I love them! They're funny—so droll."

"One of these belongs to you. Which shall it be? Mr. Mouse on the keyboard or sitting on the book?"

"The one on the bedpost," Tiffany said. "He'd be just perfect in my room. Oh, Colleen, thank you!"

I tore the page from the book and handed it to her. She took it eagerly, holding it at arm's length and examining it in delight.

She forgot the creature in the hedge and her fears for my safety. "I've got to go home now, Colleen. I can hardly wait to see how this looks over my bed. You don't mind, do you?"

"Of course not," I gave her an encouraging shove toward the door. "The rain's stopped now, but hurry! It'll probably begin again. As soon as you can, come back and tell me how it looks."

As soon as she was out of sight, I hurried outside. A glinting of pale sky showed through the veil of gray. The grass was drenched and soaked.

The milk beneath the laurel branches was untouched. I put in an exploring finger. It was faintly warm. Raindrops pelted me as I parted the branches. Two round eyes stared back at me.

"Hello, dog," I whispered. "I've brought you milk."

The creature's lips curled menacingly. Tension showed in the angle of its matted head, in its pain-laden eyes. I pushed fear aside and reached back for the bowl. Making my movements deliberately slow and reassuring, I advanced deeper into the branch-riddled cave.

A warning growl rumbled in the dog's throat. I stopped. "You've got to let me help you, dog. If you don't, you'll die."

Another growl. The creature's lips trembled, revealing its teeth. It was close—too close.

I wanted to back away. But something inside me compelled me to try to help. Cautiously I inched forward.

"Please, dog." I stopped, wondering if it might respond to a name. "Buster . . . Captain . . ." There was no response in the warning eyes. "Sea Biscuit," I said suddenly. "You'd make a good Sea Biscuit."

The dog's trembling lips seemed to relax. "Sea Biscuit," I said in a conversational tone, "you can't tell me you've been wild all your life."

I moved my knee closer, thrusting deeper inside the hedge. "Are you like me, Sea Biscuit, a ship loose from the harbor?"

My hand trembled as I placed the bowl before his nose. I watched his nostrils quiver.

"Good Sea Biscuit," I encouraged. Strangely enough, the dog responded. The fear buried deep inside his eyes lessened, the warning growls quieted.

I longed to reach out and stroke his muzzle, but wisdom beyond my own held me back. "Good Sea Biscuit," I whispered, inching backward. From the edge, I gave him one last encouraging word. "Drink it all, Sea Biscuit. Drink it all."

I wanted to peek back inside to see what Sea Biscuit was doing. Instead, I turned and went toward the house.

A dream awaited me inside, a silver moonlit scene that was a part of my immediate present. And from the past beckoned still another—a shining path that promised to shine more and more until the perfect day. I began to run.

I spent the early evening alone in my room capturing the scene my imagination had caught earlier—the jutting cliff hanging in the moonlit night, the moon, the man and woman, but most of all, the paths on the sea. The rough waves captivated me. If only my fingers would obey my will.

But the sea beneath my fingers remained lifeless. No matter how I tried, it refused to give back even a glimmer of what was inside me. At last I lay down my pencil in disgust.

"It's no use," I said aloud. "Perhaps if I had paints."

My thoughts returned to Sea Biscuit. I laid my pencil down, shoved the sketchbook beneath my pillow, and slipped into my jacket. Outside in the shadowy twilight, I parted the wet branches and peered into the dark cave-like interior. Even in the elusive light, I saw his eyes clearly. Did I imagine a faint glimmer of welcome?

"Melissa has a dog now, Sea Biscuit," I said conversationally. "He rescued her once from some fellows who were chasing her."

Sea Biscuit's eyes followed my hand movements as I reached for the bowl. Elation filled me as I noted it was empty. "Good Sea Biscuit," I encouraged. "Good dog."

Was it my imagination, or was there a faint wag of his mangy tail? I took hold of my courage and reached an uncertain hand toward his muzzle. The hair felt crusted and horrible and I swallowed hard. Emotions tugged at me as he tolerated my tentative stroking.

After a few moments I drew back and began backing out of the hedge. "I'm coming back, Sea Biscuit. I promise." I hurried into the house.

After a light supper of soup and milk, Miss Lavender turned to me. "About the diary, Colleen . . ." She played with the silver salt shaker, her fingers not quite as relaxed as her bearing.

"I haven't read it," I said. "Somehow it didn't seem quite right. It's in my room, though."

Miss Lavender's smile was gentle. "It happened so long ago. It probably means nothing."

"Of course," I agreed. I changed the conversation. "I tried to sketch a scene this afternoon," I added. "But it didn't turn out too good."

For once Miss Lavender didn't seem interested in my art. "I heard the minister's daughter," she said, "while I was resting—thinking."

I nodded. "We spent the afternoon together. I gave her the picture of the mouse swinging from the bedpost. She loved it."

Our conversation stayed in safe channels until it was time for bed. Miss Lavender held her hand out to me before she left the room. I took it, wondering at the sudden intensity in her eyes.

"About the diary, Colleen," she said in a low voice, "I want you to read it tonight—please."

I pressed her hand in assent, wondering at her emotion. What did Amelia have to say that Miss Lavender wanted me to know?

That night I lay in bed, the blanket drawn to my chin, my fingers smoothing the edges of the small black diary.

I opened it and began to read.

10 / More Than a Love Story

Amelia's story curled itself around me and transported me into the past. It was long after midnight before I turned out the light.

I lay in the darkness, the spidery handwriting still marching before my eyes. I understood now why Miss Lavender wanted me to read the diary. It was more than a love story—it was a young girl's pilgrimage toward God.

"The last summer of her life," I whispered into the stillness. "And she was young, not yet twenty-one. She didn't know she was going to die . . ."

I took a deep breath, then let it out slowly. "She grappled with all the things that count—disappointment, jealousy, hate; then love, forgiveness, acceptance.

"She came out on God's side."

I turned onto my side, plumping my pillow into fatness, trying to bury down into sleep. It was no use.

I'm glad I learned to love. I'm even glad I had to learn to do without that love. It helps me understand Calvary a little more—the loneliness Jesus must have felt when He was dying so painfully.

Loneliness coupled with a desolation flailed me. I almost wished my impish mouse would return, but he remained silent.

I turned onto my back and stared wide-eyed at the ceiling, trying to see the story from Miss Lavender's viewpoint. It must have hurt deeply when she first read Amelia's feelings.

My sister—my own sister. Why can't she see how much I care for Lawrence? Why must she constantly flirt and flaunt herself before him?

Is she made of stone? Or is she so totally wrapped up

in herself she sees nothing, feels nothing, for others—for me?

Oh, Lord, how can I learn to think your way? Teach me to love—to forgive, no matter what.

"She lived a transparent life before the Lord," I whispered, "not like me. I'm forever dodging issues, running from responsibility, from God."

I groped for the light switch. A circle of golden light illumined the black diary. *I needed to find the place Amelia wrote about Opal running—the quotation from the book she was reading.*

My eyes searched the spidery writing. *I'm reading from Hannah Whitall Smith's book, "The God of All Comfort." She writes:*

A wild young fellow brought to the Lord who became a rejoicing Christian living an exemplary life afterward was asked what he did to get converted. 'Oh,' he said, 'I did my part, and the Lord did His.'

" 'But what was your part and what was the Lord's part?'

" 'My part was to run away and the Lord's part was to run after me 'til He caught me.' "

My eyes blurred with sudden tears. The words beneath the quotation wobbled before my eyes. But I knew what they said:

Lord, that's my sister, Opal. She's running, God. Oh, Lord, catch her. Bring her back to you. . . .

I rubbed my eyes on the corner of the sheet, then turned the page. Amelia had written in words from the Bible. *"His word runneth very swiftly. . . . He sendeth out his word, and melteth them" (Psalm 147).* Then she had written, *Send out your word, Lord. Hurry! Catch my sister, Opal.*

I closed the book softly and turned off the light. *Miss Lavender had once run from God.*

A vision of her racing from God rose before my eyes. I could imagine her young with long blond hair. It streamed behind her as she ran . . . and ran . . . and ran . . .

I awoke feeling weary, almost as though I'd been running all night. Had it been part of a dream or merely the influence of Amelia's diary?

I thought about it as I brushed my own long blond hair. It reminded me of my imagined picture of Miss Lavender. How strange it must have felt to be pursued by the God of heaven.

I tried to tell her about it as we had late breakfast together. "I'm not sure what Amelia's diary meant to you, Miss Lavender. But I know what stuck with me. It was her picture of you running from God and her prayer, 'Lord, catch her. Hurry.' "

She nodded. "Her diary hurt me horribly, Colleen. I have to tell you that." For a moment her hands covered her face. Then she looked at me.

"As I read, I suddenly saw myself as I was then. And I saw something else. It was the many years I wasted running from God."

Sorrow stirred in me as I saw grief and pain in her eyes. "But you love Him now, Miss Lavender. I can see it in your words, your actions."

"I know, Colleen. But how hard I was, how rebellious! Those years I spent running can never be reclaimed. And how I hurt my sister! I never knew until now how much."

I tried to change the subject. "I noticed she wrote 'Follow the moonpath' in the margin several times. And the pendant she talked about—the one belonging to Lawrence Redgate. Has anyone ever found it?"

Miss Lavender shook her head. "No. But then nobody had any idea . . . ." Her voice faded into softness. "Remember how I told you she'd been delirious before her death? She kept saying—"

" '. . . Follow the moonpath,' " I interrupted, " 'just follow the moonpath. It leads to the sun.' But I must confess, I forgot about it until now. I was too taken up with her prayers for you—that phrase from the Psalms."

"I know," she said quietly, then pushed her chair back and stood. I looked up at her anxiously.

She smiled down at me. I was glad to see serenity in her eyes, quiet peace reflected where only moments before painful memories had shown through.

"Feel free to keep the diary for a while, Colleen. Maybe—who knows . . ." Her voice drifted from me as she carried the dishes to the sink.

I hurried to help her. As soon as I'd finished, I went back upstairs.

My sketchbook waited for me on my bedside table. I reached for my jacket, then grabbed the sketchbook, choosing to ignore the black diary.

The phone rang as I hurried through the living room. I lifted the receiver. "Hello."

"Colleen, it's me, Alan. I'm on my way to the beach. Want to go for another run?"

I hesitated only a fraction of a moment. Those waves— Alan beside me—the endless sand . . . "I'd love it," I said recklessly. "In fact, I'm on my way there right now. You could meet me just beyond the house."

Excitement trilled through me. I clutched my sketchbook tighter, then ran out the door. In only a few minutes the sea stretched before me like sullen gray glass. As I paused, a group of sea gulls flew over my head. My gaze followed them as they winged over the brooding waters.

Even as I counted them, nostalgia tugged inside me. *Seven sea gulls flying.* Those gulls reminded me of the seagull mobile in my room at home. Quite suddenly I wondered what my family was doing—Dad, Mom, Melissa, my monstrous little brother Darryl . . .

I heard footsteps behind me, felt a gentle touch on my arm, and turned to face Alan. He stood, his legs braced, grinning a genuine welcome that illuminated a face ruddy with wind and exertion.

We turned northward in unspoken consent. For some reason I didn't even try to understand. I wanted to share with him the cave I'd discovered.

Our steady, unhurried, rhythmic pace ate up the distance. I caught my second wind and ran with ease. It wasn't long before the rocky outcropping stretched before us.

"We'll have to climb!" I shouted. I took the lead and he followed, leaping rocks, balancing on ledges.

My cave loomed ahead. I bent my head and stepped inside. Alan was close behind—I could hear his heavy breathing. When I stood upright he was beside me.

We stood without words, sheltered from the wind. Alan was the first to break the silence. "It's your own little world, isn't it, Colleen? I feel honored that you would share it with me."

"I wasn't going to show it to anyone," I said brusquely. I gestured around the enclosed room. "Something about this place helps me . . ." I struggled to find words.

My gaze met his. "I think God has something for me to learn here," I said, "but I haven't quite figured it out."

I stared at him, almost expecting him to laugh or make a remark that would make me feel foolish. He did neither. Instead I saw something that looked almost like tenderness around his lips. I bit my own and averted my eyes, looking down at the hard-packed sandy floor.

"Perhaps," Alan said softly, "you need to come here often—alone with your Bible."

After that it was easy to talk. I told him about the dog holed up in the hedge and Tiffany's anxiety. I even shared my fears that I'd never be able to recapture the mood and beauty of my former seascapes. I opened my sketchbook after a while and began to make little dips and swirls that resembled waves.

Alan peered over my shoulder. "What is it you're trying to capture?" he asked. "Something besides those roaring waves?"

I tried to explain the little silver paths I'd seen in my dream. A light gleamed in Alan's eyes. "I've seen that myself!" he exclaimed. He gestured further north. "There's a viewpoint high over that way overlooking the ocean. If the winds and tides are right, you can see paths glinting in the sunshine."

"But I want moonlight," I explained. I told him about

the message entangled in the diary and the verse sampler hanging over my bed.

Alan was intrigued. "I think you might be stumbling onto a hidden secret," he said. "I wonder what the sister was trying to tell Miss Lavender."

But right then the mystery failed to capture my attention. I was too intent on sketching my ocean path.

But Alan's next words instantly grabbed my imagination. He said it almost idly, without much thought. "There's a place in the Psalms that talks about the waves clapping their hands. Can't you imagine God's hands inside those waves, bringing His palms together in a mighty boom?"

"That's it!" I cried. My fingers flew over my sketchbook. The wave I was working on suddenly came alive—and inside—a pair of clapping hands became a part of it.

"Colleen," Alan said, his face radiant. "You've got it! It's a part of the wave—God's hands—clapping with joy!"

But I knew the joy Alan felt was only a fraction of the joy welling up inside me. "I did it," I whispered. "It's something more than I've ever captured before." Awe mingled with reverence overwhelmed me. "Oh, Alan, it's a little bit like being present at creation, don't you think?"

I timidly touched his hand. "Thank you. Thank you for saying what you did."

The answering light glinting in his hazel eyes reflected the color of the waves—the sand—the rock walls encircling us. "You said God had something for you to learn here," he said. "Perhaps these waves are a part of it."

Cornish hens in earthenware containers, pumpkin pie resplendent with whipped cream, fruit salad glistening with red grapes and pineapple and garnished with walnut bits adorned the counter.

"I hope Pete appreciates this," I muttered as I folded in a dressing of mayonnaise and whipped cream.

Miss Lavender turned from the sink. "What did you say, Miss Marigold?"

"Just hoping Pete likes our Thanksgiving spread. It looks good—smells delicious."

"He's a man," she said with assurance. "Men like to eat."

I smiled in agreement. It had been that way in my childhood home too. Dad bending over the cooking pots, Mom shooing him out of the kitchen. Nostalgia swept through me.

I pushed my thoughts aside and concentrated on the salad. The last few days had been busy with housecleaning and grocery shopping for Thanksgiving extras.

Miss Lavender insisted I accept a check for being her companion and helper, so I'd had the excitement of purchasing a set of oils and turning the extra upstairs room into a studio of sorts. The furniture was sparse: an easel, a card table to hold my paints, a single chair.

There, my seascape was growing. Instead of a night scene of silver and moonlight, I'd decided on noonday brilliance. Clear blues and vivid greens reflected the clapping hands, turning them into an expression of pure joy. Every time I worked on it I felt something deep inside transforming me.

It was that way with Sea Biscuit too. He still lay hidden in the shrubbery, but he was changing. The last time I'd fed him I'd seen the faintest movement in his tail. I could hardly wait until I could coax him into the light of day.

"Just goes to show you what love and food will do," I said softly.

Miss Lavender raised her eyebrows. "What did you say?"

"Love and food in just the right combination do a lot, don't you think?"

A whimsical smile flashed across her lips. "Especially if it's a man!"

I bent over the salad, trying to hide the crimson rushing into my cheeks. I was sure she was thinking of Pete, but I knew who had occupied my thoughts the past few days.

I couldn't understand why every time something happened, I found my thoughts telling Alan about it in great detail. If he had been around he'd have heard about Sea Biscuit's response, what the room I called my studio looked like, how my "Clapping Hands" painting was developing stroke by stroke into a seascape of beauty.

The doorbell rang and I went to answer it. Pete stood on the steps, loaded down with a giant golden chrysanthemum. He held it out to me with an expectant boyish smile.

My heart tipped treacherously. "Why, Pete! It's beautiful!"

The deep cleft in his chin deepened. His blue eyes looked bluer than ever. "It's for the dearest girl I know." His voice lowered. "And that's you, Colleen."

"Oh, Pete!" I protested. I thrust my nose into the flower's golden depths, hoping he wouldn't see the confusion in my face. His arm slipped around my waist, increasing my consternation.

I stepped away from him, motioning kitchenward with the chrysanthemum. "I hope you've brought something for Miss Lavender. After all, she's your hostess."

The intensity of Pete's gaze didn't escape me. "Don't worry," he said, "I haven't forgotten."

I was conscious of his hand on the small of my back as we walked into the dining room.

I glanced at his face quickly, noted his gaze sweep over the place settings of old rose china and beige lace napkins.

"Just us?" he asked.

Something in his tone made me bristle. "Who else did you expect?"

Pete pursed his lips thoughtfully. The cleft in his chin deepened. "I just wondered," he mused. "You and that preacher guy seemed kind of close."

I whirled to face him, hating the way my chin lifted in haughty defiance, the feeling revealed in the iciness of my tone. "I thought we talked about this earlier. Besides, Pete Erickson, there's a lot you don't know about a lot of people—especially Alan Nichols!"

Pete's eyes narrowed. "Colleen—"

"As for Alan," I flared, "I've neither seen nor talked with him for four days. He hasn't bothered to come by to see how my new painting is progressing, let alone—"

I stopped abruptly as sudden understanding dawned in Pete's eyes. "So that's the way the wind blows," he said softly.

I refused to say another word. I shoved the golden chrysanthemum onto the corner table and hurried to the kitchen to help Miss Lavender.

11 / The Shepherd of the Sea

Afterward I wondered why I'd responded to Pete as I had. Did it really matter so much that Alan hadn't tried to get in touch with me since the day we'd shared those moments in the cave above the sea?

I bent over the colors in my palette. Only a bit more shading and the hands in the waves would have a perfect balance of subtlety and light. A longing welled up inside me. I wanted Alan to see my seascape in its finished glory.

A darker blue here, a touch of turquoise there; I stood back, my brush in hand. My painting was all I had dreamed it would be, and more. I knew I'd caught a tiny glimpse of God's majesty and joy in His great creation. Perhaps it even portrayed something of His power.

A hush fell over my innermost being. I plunged my brush into the cleaner, then covered my eyes.

"Oh, God," I whispered, "you are all glorious, holy, powerful. I can't understand how I, so ugly and rebellious, could even be loved by you."

Into my mind rose a picture of Miss Lavender running from the great God of heaven. He was coming after her—only it was me now. I could feel His great, gentle hands cup themselves around my spirit. I could almost feel His breath stir against the back of my neck.

Lord, I want to know you better. Not just as the great hound of heaven, or even as the awesome, mighty God. I'd like to know you as the Shepherd who loves and cares for His flock.

I don't know how long I sat still, my heart yearning after Him, my hands covering my eyes. When I uncovered my face, dusk had come. A soft darkness obscured my painting. But the spirit of the waves was with me in the room, whispering quiet words from the great Creator.

I had a sudden longing to read Amelia's diary again, to discover what she'd learned. But something held me back, and I knew it wasn't mere reluctance to intrude into her life. Something deeper plagued me.

Lord, I'm afraid to really give myself totally to you. I've tried so many times to be the person you wanted—my parents wanted. Always, I've failed.

I stood up. *I would go to the sea, let it talk to me.* I hurried downstairs, stopping only long enough to grab a jacket.

The night swept in windy glory around me. Great broken clouds scuttled across the expanse of awakening stars. The sea pounded against the sand, its mighty roar filling my spirit with a disquieting unrest.

As I came closer I saw it was high tide. Great white breakers flung themselves close to where the grassy dunes met the flattened expanse of sandy beach.

I rushed to meet the waves, then turned, running in the narrow channel between the dunes and sea. The flailing waves filled the air with spray, dampening my face, misting my hair, I ran eagerly, my thoughts keeping pace with my running feet.

"Great Star Shepherd, Shepherd of the Sea, come to me . . ."

The wind snatched my words from my lips, tossed them to the roiling water. "I've tried to live the Christian life on my own too many times, Lord!" I shouted. "And I'm still trying! But it's no use! I need a different attitude toward my family—Pete—you. If you love me, catch me the way you did Miss Lavender. Change me."

The channel before me narrowed, reminding me of a path. *Known unto Him are the paths of the sea. The path of the just is as a shining light, that shineth more and more unto the perfect day.*

"I'm not a 'just' person, God! I've sinned! Not just once—many times! I need to be forgiven!"

A wave crashed close, soaking me to my knees. I turned

to the grassy dune. Sand stuck to my tennis shoes and the bottom of my jeans, but I went forward, climbing higher and higher. At the top I turned. The damp sand between me and the sea glistened a moonlit path to the water's edge.

I caught my breath. Beyond the breaking waves I saw a path through the sea. It was a silver path that led upward, into the sky. Before my gaze, the stars seemed to lower. A great red one dipped close to the thundering waves.

"Mars," I murmured, "the god of war." *Like the war raging inside my own rebellious heart.*

My eyes misted with sudden tears. I swallowed hard and squeezed them shut. When I opened them I saw a skiff of fog had moved over the water, blotting out the crimson star.

I turned. To my left rose a cliff. My imagination sketched in a woman and man silhouetted against the stars. I blinked. I could visualize a multitude of silver paths on the water, carved by the wind, silvered by moonlight, designed by the Master Creator.

Then the wind molded the fog into a figure walking on the waves. The Great Shepherd of the Sea moved toward the figures on the cliff, His arms outstretched, His robes blowing. An involuntary cry tore from my lips. He seemed to turn toward me and I lifted my own arms in response to Him, my spirit exulting.

I knew exactly what my next seascape would be. But I knew something else that was much, much more important: the Shepherd of the Sea, the God I'd been running from for so long, had come for me. Even though I couldn't really understand, I knew He'd caught me close in His great loving arms.

I was through running. More than anything else, I wanted to be close to Him forever.

I turned homeward. I was eager to begin my new painting, but even more eager to learn more about my Shepherd.

A dark shape standing in front of the hedge by the house halted my running feet. I skidded to a stop. Sea Biscuit stood there, his huge head held high.

"Sea Biscuit!" I gasped, "is it really you?" I advanced

slowly, hesitantly, holding out my hand.

He was much taller than I had thought. His massive head came almost to my waist. I wondered what kind of dog he was.

He stood still as my faltering hand touched the matted hair between his ears. In the faint light coming from the porch, I was able to discern large crusted areas on his upper legs and abdomen.

"You poor thing," I sighed. "No wonder you've lain so still. Whatever did you tangle with?" I examined his stomach gently while he stood immobile, enduring my touch.

"You need a bath and more food." My hand returned to his head. I looked deep into his eyes and saw something beautiful and trusting in them.

A hard lump bumped into my throat. "Poor prodigal dog," I soothed, patting him gently, "I'm glad you've come out of your hedge. We're going to be friends, aren't we? Friends." When I stepped onto the porch, Sea Biscuit was beside me.

My dreams that night were a tangled skein of endless threads that made no sense whatever. Amelia's sampler dangled over the back of a huge dog running endlessly down a path. Silver threads unraveled from the embroidered piece, working its way around and around the poor dog's legs.

I was glad when I wakened to daylight streaming through the window. I got up quickly, putting my confused dream aside. I wanted to see how Sea Biscuit had fared through the night. Would he still be curled up on the old blanket I'd left for him on the porch?

He was. I delighted in the welcome shining from his brown eyes and went to him at once, putting my hand on his broad forehead.

"Well, Sea Biscuit, I'm not sure what Miss Lavender will say, but I know what I think: you're my dog now, for better or worse. And that means a bath."

As I looked at his huge frame, I wondered how I'd manage it. It turned out to be easier than I expected.

Miss Lavender wasn't repulsed by his huge, gaunt scarred body. "I'm glad he's found you, Colleen," she said. "He needs lots of love and tender care." She gave me a searching look. "He'll get that from you, I'm sure."

We decided a sponge bath would be the answer to the dirt problem. I brought out a dishpan of warm water and set it close to Sea Biscuit. Using a large sponge, I cleaned him thoroughly. He endured it nobly, even seemed to enjoy it.

Afterward I took a fresh sponge and a basin of betadine solution and gently cleansed his injured areas. He only winced once, then stood trembling. It was as though he understood I was trying to help him. When I finished, he went back to his blanket and lay down, closing his eyes.

I left food with him and hurried upstairs. The paths of the sea were calling me, but there was something else even more important. I kept remembering the words Alan had read the night of the harvest dinner—something about God binding up broken legs or wounds. He'd read it from somewhere in the Old Testament.

But try as I could, I couldn't find it. At last I turned to the familiar twenty-third Psalm. From there I went to Luke and read the story of the lost sheep—the lost boy—the lost coin.

So many lost things, I thought. *Like me, far from God, wandering, searching, confused, alone . . . Then joy—suddenly found—caught by the Great Shepherd.*

That afternoon, Tiffany and I spent time together admiring Sea Biscuit. His once matted coat was smoother now and I was surprised to see golden glimmers hidden in the dull hair across his shoulders.

"He must have been a beautiful dog once," Tiffany mused. "I didn't think you'd ever tame him though, Colleen. He seemed so wild."

I smiled. "He just needed encouragement—and a great big dose of tender loving care."

"He's a lot different than the dog Dad described as lunging out at you." She looked up at me, her thoughtful eyes examining me. "You seem different too, Colleen. Is it because you're able to paint again?''

"Partly. But mostly I think it's that I've stopped running.''

Tiny frowns appeared on Tiffany's forehead. She wrinkled her nose in an endearing little gesture. "Running?''

"From God,'' I explained. "You see, Tiffany, when I came here I was really running away—from my family, my responsibilities, but most of all my God.'' I stopped, not sure how to explain.

"Go on,'' Tiffany urged.

"It was Amelia's diary that did it, I guess. She's Opal's sister, the one who died. Do you know about it?''

Tiffany shook her head.

"Let me explain,'' I said. Quickly I told her of my discovery of the diary and what I could of Miss Lavender's discomfort.

But Tiffany was more interested in my allusions to the moonpath than to either Amelia's spiritual pilgrimage or Miss Lavender's feelings.

"Do you think Miss Lavender would let me read it?'' she exclaimed. "It sounds so exciting.''

"There was apparently a lost love and a lost pendant,'' I said.

Tiffany bounced on her heels. "Ooh,'' she squealed, "hidden treasure—a moonpath—a lost love! It sounds wonderful!''

I couldn't match her enthusiasm. "Her diary meant more to me than that, Tiffany. It brought me to the place where I saw my need of the Lord in a new way.''

Immediately Tiffany grew serious. "I'm sorry,'' she said. "Tell me.''

"When I was a little girl I decided to accept Jesus' death as taking the punishment I deserved,'' I explained hesitantly. "And I knew that His resurrection meant I would live after I died. . . . But this is different. I've made a deeper commitment. I want to be with Him—share His life in a new way, really become His disciple. I almost feel something inside me will die if I don't get to know Him better.''

Tiffany nodded wisely. "You should talk to my parents. They're wise. They'd show you how to get close to Him."

I stood suddenly. "Tiffany, would you like to see my clapping hands? I just finished it."

"Ooh," she squealed again, "a painting! Is it more elves—or mice?"

"No." I smiled down at her. "It's a seascape, Tiffany. And it's beautiful. You'll love it."

I was right. Tiffany was captivated by the hands inside the waves. She knew without my telling her just whose hands they were.

"I can't understand how you did it, Colleen. I just don't understand," she said over and over again.

I tried to explain to her how it was something I saw with my inside vision. "It's just there. But if it isn't, if I can't see it, well, then I can't paint it."

Tiffany shook her head, gesturing out the window. "But that's impossible, Colleen. Why, that would mean you could paint anything you could see, and you told me yourself that for a while you couldn't paint."

I wished I could explain it to her. How could the unseen things within me be as real as the outward world? "It's a bit like faith, I guess. I can't explain it completely, but it's real."

That seemed to satisfy her, although she was still shaking her head as we went downstairs. Miss Lavender stood at the bottom of the steps, smiling up at us.

"Telephone," she said. "It's for you."

I raised my eyebrows into a question and picked up the receiver. My heart dipped. I recognized that voice.

It was Alan.

12 / A New Day Dawns

I stood before the open closet examining each of my outfits. My eyes lingered on my cream-colored blazer suit. Coupled with my new swirly green and blue blouse, it just might do.

I reached for it with sudden decisiveness and held it up to my face, peering critically into the mirror. Did it really bring out the sea colors in my eyes the way I thought it had when I bought it?

Anticipation mingled with doubt rushed through me. When Alan had asked me to accompany him to his friend's art show, he'd also said, "Let's make an occasion of it. After we've toured the place, we could have dinner at the Ox Bow Inn."

The art show I could handle; it was dinner at an elegant restaurant that stirred up butterflies. I laid the blouse and suit on the bed, picked up my robe and went downstairs for my shower. As the water pounded and invigorated me, I thought about the week behind me.

It had been special in its own quiet way. First had come Alan's invitation to the art display. Then Sherry suggested that she and I meet each week for a time of sharing and Bible study to establish the new commitment I'd made with my Lord.

Already I could tell it was what I needed. Sherry's idea for knowing God was simple—spend time with Him. She outlined a Bible reading guide and challenged me to write down what I felt God was saying to me.

My adventure in learning to know Jesus intimately had already begun to equal Amelia's. My spiritual journal was a simple spiral notebook written in pencil; hers was cloth bound, done in elegant silver script. But both of them reflected our own individual growth.

Excitement coursed through me every time I read Amelia's notebook. Would my own someday have something to say to another generation? The thought stirred awe and a certain reluctance in me.

As the silver paths of the sea unfolded on my canvas, I felt much the same sensations. The moon and the cliff grew beneath my fingertips, a part of a majestic creation that wasn't me—yet somehow was. Tomorrow I would begin work on the Shepherd's open arms, reaching out to hold me.

Back in my room, I dried my hair to silky perfection, then slipped into my new blouse and suit. I turned in front of the mirror, pulling my stomach flat, smoothing my blouse. "Well, young lady," I said to my mirrored reflection, "you don't look half bad."

I caught up my purse and coat and went downstairs. The doorbell rang at exactly 3 p.m.

Alan and an exuberant Sea Biscuit stood together on the porch, anticipation and eagerness written on both their faces.

"I can't believe that dog," I exclaimed, "once he decided to love me, he took on the whole world!"

Alan laughed. "Shouldn't be hard to do, I imagine."

A flush rose into my cheeks. I wasn't sure which he meant wasn't hard to do—love me or take on the whole world. To cover my confusion I reached down to scratch behind Sea Biscuit's ears.

"He loves this," I said.

Alan grinned. "It's part of the love package, isn't it, Sea Biscuit?" He squatted beside the dog. "He's almost healed, isn't he?"

I nodded. "He feels better too. His coat is getting slicker and healthier."

Alan stood again. "Where's Miss Lavender?" he asked.

"It's her naptime," I explained.

"Then shall we?" he asked. He gave me his arm with old-fashioned gentlemanly charm. I took it with what I hoped was equal grace. He guided me to his white Toyota pickup, opening the door with a flourish.

"Here's where the charm evaporates," he stated apologetically. "There just isn't any way I can get you inside with grace and dignity."

I giggled as I climbed up. Tossing my hair over my shoulders, I looked down at him from the high seat. "I must admit pickups and suits really *don't* go together."

"You're telling me?" He closed the door and went around to the other side. "Remind you of another day?" he asked as he slid behind the wheel.

I nodded. "The first time we met—almost two months ago."

"In a way it seems like ages—then again almost yesterday. I'll be speaking tomorrow at church, Colleen. Will you be there?"

"Yes. I haven't told you yet, Alan, but my life is different since I saw you last. I've made a new commitment to Jesus Christ. I've even followed your suggestion and taken my Bible down to the rock cave."

He looked at me searchingly. "It was Amelia's diary that did it, wasn't it?"

I nodded. "Most of all it was her description of Miss Lavender running from God that grabbed me. I saw a picture of myself. And then—" I paused. I didn't know how to tell him about my Shepherd of the sea.

"Go on. What next?"

"God caught me. I climbed to the top of a dune, and—and—He came to me, put His arms around me. I can't explain it—except I know it happened."

I leaned forward, cupping my chin in my hands. "That wasn't all, Alan. When the fog blew in from the sea, I saw the illusion of a Shepherd with outstretched arms coming toward me. I know it was only fog, and yet He was so real. And I'd been praying, 'Lord, if you love me, come to me.' "

Alan leaned toward me and gave me a quick squeeze. "He does love you," he said. "Now continue."

"It's the theme for my new seascape, Alan. That night I suddenly saw the paths on the sea I'd been trying so hard to capture." I gestured to my left. "There's a cliff there, with a man and girl silhouetted on it. There's moonlight and starlight, and beyond the white-capped waves the paths are beautiful and plain—easy to see, easy to follow.

"A skiff of fog is blowing in over the ocean. It will be like the clapping hands. People won't realize they're there at first. But as they look they'll discover the Shepherd walking toward them on a path in the sea." I lowered my voice. "His arms will be outstretched—the wind will blow His hair, His robe.

"The theologians won't like it much, Alan. They'll think I'm a flighty mystic."

Alan turned on the ignition. "They'll think nothing of the kind. And if they do, what does it matter? God has given you a unique way of looking at your world. Don't fight it, Colleen. Trust Him."

He turned onto the street. "Speaking of silver paths, which we were, Tiffany is all excited about Amelia's mystery—the one she alluded to in her diary."

"Yes, I know. 'Follow the moonpath' and then that part where she talks about the pendant Lawrence gave her, and hiding it. But it was so long ago. Over half a century!

"Alan, do you remember the night of the harvest dinner? That verse you quoted keeps coming into my mind, but I can't find it."

Alan caught his lower lip between his teeth. "The 23rd Psalm, wasn't it? Didn't I talk about God as the restorer, the healer of the bruised and hurting?"

"Yes. But you read something about God bandaging up the wounded, taking into His arms the broken and the injured."

"Oh, that's in Ezekiel. God said He'd be a Shepherd to Israel, that He would heal them and restore them."

"That's it!" I cried. "I've been looking and looking! You see, it's like me. I needed to be healed of my hurts and rebellion, my restlessness and fear of responsibility. I needed to find rest inside His arms." My voice lowered. "I still do."

"I'll find the reference for you. It's a beautiful verse, full of comfort."

After that we talked of other things, like the vine maples that hung their tresses in canopies overhead, the sea gulls that flew low over the highway . . .

I was surprised when we turned off into a long driveway. "Your friend must live back in the boonies!" I exclaimed. "It's an odd place to hold an art exhibit."

But the big red barn standing alone in a large field was surrounded by cars. Alan pulled up alongside a sleek green coupe and stopped.

I looked around dubiously as I stepped onto the rutted field. "Not quite the place for city shoes and suits," I remarked.

"Not yet," he agreed. "But wait. The Ox Bow Inn is elegance itself."

The barn was tall and lofty, with huge beams. As my eyes became accustomed to its dim interior, I saw paintings propped against bales of hay.

Eagerly I drew closer, my artist's eye examining them for mood and detail: a girl carrying a bucket of foaming milk, a child digging in the sand, another encircled in his mother's arm.

"He has a love for children," I surmised. "And the country."

A man stepped from behind a bale. His dark brown eyes looked at me intently, his brows drawn together in a deep scowl. Instinctively I drew back.

Alan touched my arm gently, then said, "Colleen, this is my friend, Ken. Ken, this is Colleen."

A light flashed in the man's dark eyes, admiration replacing the scowl. "Ah, yes, the artist—the real artist." He said it quietly, almost reverently. I took another step backward.

"I've wanted to meet you," he said.

"You must be mistaking me for someone else. You—I don't think you understand—I only do fun things, cartoons, fanciful creatures. And dabble a little in oils."

"Show her the painting, Ken," Alan said softly.

"This way," Ken said.

Alan and I left the surge of people and followed the artist into a small back room at the rear of the barn. I caught the clean strong whiff of straw and hay, noted a beam of sunlight filled with dancing dust motes. *That could work into my fantasy series,* I thought. I visualized a tiny Tinker Bell chasing a gleaming, almost unseen speck, trying to capture it for fairy dust with which to sprinkle Wendy and her brothers.

Alan tugged at my hand. "You're dreaming, Colleen. Look." He pulled me in front of a canvas resting against an unused cow stall.

A shaft of sunshine rested on the painting, highlighting pink clouds and pink-tipped waves. I clapped my hands together and stepped closer.

"My painting!" I cried. "The one of Melissa and me running! But it can't be!" Tears blurred my eyes. I covered my face with my hands.

"Colleen, I didn't mean—to tamper," Alan said with concern. "Is it ruined for you?"

I uncovered my tear-stained face. "You don't understand," I whispered, "these aren't sad tears." I reached out and took Alan's hand, lifted my brimming eyes to his. "These tears are for joy. The sunrise, the footprints. It's so perfect—so beautiful."

I turned to the man with the dark, fervent eyes. "We're running into the sea," I explained, "into a brand new day, flecked with promise. And I—I thought it was gone forever."

"Thank you—thank you for doing whatever you did to restore this painting. It's more than just a picture." I touched my heart. "There's a piece of me inside it."

"It belongs to you," Ken said. He touched Alan's arm. "This man brought it to me and asked if I could fix it up like new."

"He did all I asked, and more," Alan explained.

I nodded. "It wasn't quite finished, but it is now. You did a master job, Ken."

Again Ken pointed to Alan. "I did it for him. He did something for me I'll never forget. The night of the storm, he gave me back my son—risked his life for my little boy. I owe much to Alan and—"

"Thank you, Ken," Alan interrupted. "You've given me more than a beautiful painting to return to my friend. You've given me a precious moment."

But I wanted to learn more. "You're more than an artist aren't you, Ken? You're a restorer of damaged paintings?"

The thick dark brows drew together like airplane wings. The intense foreign eyes beneath them glowed. "Yes. Oddly enough, my first love is restoration. I only dabble in painting my own canvases when I run out of the other." He leaned toward me. "Your work was a delight to my soul. You are talented far beyond most artists. Someday . . ." He shrugged expressively.

Alan was carrying my seascape through the door, drawing a crowd after him. Eagerly I pressed my advantage, pulling Ken out of Alan's hearing. "Your son," I whispered, still tugging on his hand. "How did Alan save him?"

"Oh, it was beautiful. My son was caught under a beam and I wasn't strong enough to move it. I panicked, I tell you. I got in my car and raced to the highway. Your man was driving toward me. I braked to a stop and shouted, waving my arms like a maniac. He followed me to my boy, risked his own life beneath that beam. He didn't have to, but he did."

Like Jesus did, I thought. *And Ken called Alan my man.* Joy welled up inside me.

"I'd like to see more of your work while I'm here," I said.

Happiness flooded Ken's dark face. "Your wish pleases me. Come."

The next hour was a confused jumble of too many paintings, too many people. But Alan and I enjoyed it, and it made our time in the Ox Bow that much more special.

The waiters in dark dinner jackets, the soft music, the sparkling apple cider all joined to make our evening a glistening memory. I knew I would never forget this day with the red barn, foreign Ken, and Alan.

It was flattening to return to the real world of darkened streets, white Toyotas and Miss Lavender's little house behind the hedge. But another moment just as precious waited for me.

Alan got out and opened the back of the pickup. He lifted out my sunrise of pink clouds and barefoot prints and carried it inside.

As he set it against Amelia's organ, I had a sudden longing to see it upstairs in my studio, close to the clapping hands. He must have read the desire in my eyes, for he said, "Do you want it in your studio?"

I nodded and gestured toward the stairs, leading the way up the narrow steps. Alan stepped inside the little room and looked around. Quickly I moved ahead, tossing a cloth over my unfinished paths of the sea.

Alan had eyes only for the clapping hands. "They're all your sketches promised, only more," he said.

Once again he stepped back and looked at them intently. "Colleen, how do you make one know that those waves are alive and full of song? That they carry a message as surely as my sermons do—yet more beautifully."

"No!" I objected. "God's Word is much, much more. Your sermons are powerful, filled with truth. They grab my heart—while my little sketches, seascapes, are just reflections."

I gestured toward the painting. "For me, words create pictures, moods. They begin to fill me till I feel as though I'll burst if I can't let it out. Except the beauty I paint is never quite as radiant as what I see. And I have to see it before I can paint it." My voice lowered. "I have to see."

"Colleen." It was only my name softly spoken, but it made the air tremble. I looked at him. What was there about this man that touched my heart?

His next words pushed the magic back, restoring me to the everyday world. "May I have the honor of naming this painting?"

"Please," I said. "I would be honored."

" 'Creation Joy.' Does it suit?"

"It's perfect.—That says everything I want it to."

He gestured toward the easel. "And that one—let's see— that could be called, umm, let's see . . ."

I didn't respond to his hint for a better look at the shrouded painting.

"That one's already named: 'The Shepherd of the Sea.' "

I picked up my pink sunrise and set it beside the clapping hands. "This one?"

" 'A New Beginning,' or 'A New Day Dawns.' What do you think, Colleen, does either fit?"

I could only nod in agreement. "They both do," I said. "A new day, a new life, a new beginning . . ."

13 / Silver Paths

A north wind scuttled around the corners of the gabled roof. It pressed through the windowpanes, wrapping the studio in coldness. Even though I wore sweaters and thick leg warmers, I was cold, my fingers icy. I laid my brush down and blew on them, trying to coax more warmth and feeling.

I looked out the window. In spite of the round, gold moon, the clear sky gave the illusion of harshness. *You're not like the soft, silvery moonlight in my painting,* I thought. *But it doesn't matter—that softness is inside me. I can feel it, see those silver paths, my Shepherd . . .*

He'd taken longer to paint then I had anticipated, but I was delighted with the results. His robe blew behind Him in exuberance and enthusiasm. Even His hair expressed action, delighting me with its movement.

The silver path beneath His feet quivered with light. It wasn't just light from the moon and stars. It came from Him.

With quick decisiveness I shoved my brush into the cleaner and ran downstairs. Miss Lavender sat close to the fireplace, savoring the pulsing heat, her crochet hook moving in and out of her work with quick silver flashes. She looked up as I came in.

"I was about to come up to see if you were all right. It must be icy up there."

"It is." I held my hands toward the softly whispering flames. The warmth felt heavenly on my hands.

"Strange," Miss Lavender mused, "for it to be so cold so early. Usually we don't have weather like this until after Christmas, if then."

I nodded. "It's funny—two weeks before and so cold."

"Have you decided yet whether you're going home for

Christmas?'' she asked, looking at me searchingly. ''You'll need to decide soon.''

But I could only shake my head. ''I don't know what I want. A part of me says, 'Go home. Stop thinking about yourself.' ''

''And the other part?''

''It still holds back, says, 'Not yet. Give yourself—and them—time.' '' I sighed and ran my fingers through my hair. ''Funny, in a way there's nothing I long more to do.''

''Has Pete's suggestion that you live independently, go to art school, confused you?''

''I don't know,'' I said hesitantly. ''I'd be a liar if I said I haven't thought about it. Pete could be right, you know. Even though his motive of wanting me to fit into a mold is all wrong—at least I've come to see it that way—a career and art school *is* worth thinking about.''

''And Alan,'' she pursued, ''what does he think?''

''I don't know,'' I said honestly. ''Sherry thinks I should go home for Christmas—and so does Jack. And Tiffany looks at me with those big brown eyes and says, 'But, Colleen, they'll miss you so!' And they will. I'd be less than honest to say they won't!''

I knelt beside her chair and impulsively pressed my head against her lap. Her hand was gentle on my hair, her words few. ''Just follow the moonpath, my dear. Follow the moonpath.''

I knew what she meant. The path of the Shepherd shone with His own special guiding light. If I really wanted to follow Him, He'd show me what to do. But I had to be willing—*really willing*. I thought back to the night I'd visualized my Shepherd stretching His arms wide for me. Following Him had seemed simple then.

Before I turned out my light that night, I looked at the sampler. ''Follow the moonpath—just follow the moonpath. . . .'' I pulled my bathrobe tightly around me to ward off the chill and put my feet on the bare floor.

The floor creaked as I walked across the room, my eyes examining the stitches, searching for some hidden meaning.

I fingered it, then lifted it from the nail. The sampler appeared to be mounted on heavy cardboard, the back discolored with old water stains. I wondered if there had once been a leak in the room. I turned the sampler over—gold-green leaves, gleaming path . . .

I noticed that the cloth was beginning to pull away from the corners. My fingers prodded the loosened area gently, carefully. My heart clumped with excitement as I felt a slight thickness in one corner.

Did I dare? I laid the sampler on the bed and drew on a pair of thick wool socks. I padded down the stairs softly. I wanted to find a small, pointed object with which to pry the cloth free without damaging the sampler.

Returning from the kitchen with a paring knife, I inserted the blade under the cloth where the slight bulge pushed upward on the cloth. The material lifted easily. I slipped my fingers underneath.

A small piece of yellow folded paper tumbled into my palm. For a moment apprehension trembled my hands. *Another voice from the past? What would this one say?*

But this "voice" was strangely garbled. Lines swung across it, making no sense whatever. Squares of odd designs, a circle, an X . . .

I bent over it, trying to discover some kind of ordered design from the drawing. *It could be graphic art—or even some modern rendition of someone's wild feelings,* I thought. *Or a map.*

The paper crackled under my touch. *When did modern art come into vogue,* I wondered. *Amelia's time? or later?*

I put the paper inside the black diary. Later I would ask Miss Lavender.

The smell of crisp, clean air touched my nostrils before I even opened my eyes. *Snow,* I thought. *It can't be. Not on the beach!*

But it was. I stood at my window and looked down at a changed world. Fairy tufts of white flocked the laurel hedge. The fallen beanpoles in the neighbor's yard had been transformed into silver chalices overnight.

It's like God's grace, I marveled. *He takes something ugly and in a moment transforms it into a work of art.*

Sudden joy whirled through me. I longed to go out and smell the newborn world, touch the snow's cold beauty, roll it beneath my fingertips. I hurried into my warmest clothes— a cherry red turtleneck sweater, blue jeans, heavy wool socks. I topped it all with the thick-lined jacket my parents had sent, then donned a red scarf to match my sweater and my mood.

Sea Biscuit rushed to meet me, exulting in my presence and in the crisp coldness so alien to the Oregon coast. "It's snow, Sea Biscuit!" I cried. "Do you have it where you come from?"

We ran together into the yard. I stopped to scoop up a handful, playfully pressing it close to Sea Biscuit's nose. He snorted in disgust and backed away. I laughed as he pranced backward, his tail arched high like a flag.

"Colleen!"

I turned. Pete stood at the edge of the path, expectancy written across his handsome face. He held out his hand. "I've never been to the beach in the snow," he said. "I wanted to go with you."

As I took his hand I said, "I've never seen snow here before either. Somehow rainy Oregon and snowy beaches don't fit."

"They will now," Pete grinned. "I don't think that dog likes snow after all," he said, gesturing toward Sea Biscuit.

I watched my huge blundering friend skulk onto the porch, his tail between his legs. "But he was loving it," I mourned. "I wonder what happened." I turned and ran after him.

Sea Biscuit lay on his blanket in the corner, his great brown eyes pleading with me, begging me to understand. It wasn't the snow he was running from, I realized. He was jealous of Pete!

I laid my hand on his broad head and bent over him, murmuring endearment that didn't make a great deal of sense.

I shook a warning at Pete as he mounted the steps.

"It's all right, Sea Biscuit," I soothed. "I'm going to the beach with Pete, but that doesn't mean I like him best. You're number one." Gently I smoothed the silk behind his ears, patted his broad shoulder. "I'll be back soon. We'll run together."

I gave him one last parting pat and went to join Pete.

The snowy beach welcomed us. We marveled at the snow-covered sand, at the waves rising to meet it, their white foam crests creating scallops, melting the snow into the sand then rushing back to the sea.

We ran together on the pure, untouched white, our footprints making patterns, zigzagging into surprising little contours and unexpected twists.

"I've never run on snow-covered sand before!" I cried. "It's marvelous—the air is wonderful!"

I stopped, taking great gulps of the cold snow and salt-cleansed air. The ocean stretched before me, overhung by heavy snow-laden clouds. A sea gull winged lazily overhead, his gray and white feathers dull against the gleaming white snow-tufted hill beyond.

We turned north. Our running feet reminded me of another day, another man beside me. *Alan.* The thought stabbed me, stopped my running feet. *Alan—Sea Biscuit.*

Pete slowed, turned toward me. "Come on!" he shouted.

I shook my head. "In a minute. Just give me time to enjoy this!" I waved my arms wide, trying to take in the magic panorama of sea, sky and snow. "It's beautiful! To think I've never connected ocean and snow together before!"

"There're lots of things you've not put together before," he said meaningfully.

My precious moment was destroyed. Pete took several steps toward me.

I drew back. He seemed to sense my changed mood, for he turned oceanward, running close to the waves. Once again he turned and extended his arms. "Come!" he shouted over the ocean's roar.

The picture he made standing there touched something inside me. Pete's footprints led seaward. Were they leading me away from God's direction? Away from Mom and Dad, Melissa, Darryl? Was there another path out of sight, indistinct now, yet waiting for me?

But my Shepherd's footprints led to a silver path, glistening with glory, created especially for me. *The path of the just is as a shining light that shines more and more until the perfect day.*

Shepherd of the Sea, the snow. You're going before me right now. I can trust you to guide me! I can trust who I am and all I have to you.

A flurry of snow swirled around my face. I ran toward the waves. And if Pete saw the joy on my face and thought it was for him, well, never mind. Someday he'd understand.

All that day snow fell. Miss Lavender and I sat together by the fireplace in the living room and marveled at it.

"If this keeps up, we'll have a white Christmas!" I exclaimed.

But she shook her head. "It'll be gone in a few days," she prophesied. "You'll see."

She was right. On the evening of the third day of snow, the wind changed. A welcome warmth accompanied by a gentle breeze stole up from the south.

The evergreen trees dislodged their snowy bundles, the lawn became a patchwork quilt of white and weary green. The eaves were alive with sound—drips and splashes and gurgles. The cars on the street no longer moved like stealthy phantoms. Their engines roared, their wheels splashed. All Oregon's wet glory had returned.

By midnight the wind gained momentum. It clawed against my window, stirring the curtains, seeking entrance. The house came alive with strange creaks and groans. Something heavy blew against the roof, rolling violently.

Memories of the October storm we'd recently weathered drove me from my bed. Rain splashed the glass, running the rivulets against the pane, blurring the view. I could barely see the outline of twisted trees.

The wind shrieked like a tortured animal. Something slammed into the wall, like the sound of a falling ladder. Cold fear settled into my stomach. I shivered, almost envying Miss Lavender's ability to sleep through anything.

"There's nothing that can be done," I told myself as I crept back into bed, pulling the blanket over my head, shutting out the noise. Even as I spoke to my Shepherd, a picture came to me. I saw Him—strong, powerful, His hands placed on the top of Miss Lavender's house. His hair blew in the wind, His robe streamed around Him. But still He stayed, protecting.

A quiet calm came over my spirit. I needed to capture that picture and show it to the world.

I folded back the sheet, slid my feet onto the floor and padded softly to my studio across the hall. For a brief moment I gave my attention to the finished paintings propped against the wall; the joy in the clapping hands, the mystery of the silver paths of the sea drew me.

Strange how different those two paintings were from the one of Melissa and me running in the pink dawn. I was amazed how much I had changed.

Nostalgia stirred inside me. Christmas was coming; I pictured my family in church—remembered shepherds, angels, the baby Jesus. *Would Darryl be a shepherd again this year? And what of Melissa? Would she and her new friend, Elaine, be singing carols? Shopping together? Would they giggle over silly, inexpensive gift selections the way she and I used to do?*

I stepped closer to the painting, scrutinizing it carefully. Those ceaseless waves rolling in on the beach were like the waves in my life—ebbing, flowing, urging me forward, then pulling me back, sometimes threatening, then calming.

I'd almost forgotten about the storm and the picture I wanted to capture. I grabbed my sketchbook, caught up my sketching pencil.

The storm roared its rage and I listened. I sank into the only chair, my pencil flying across the white page. My Shepherd, the strong and powerful God I was learning to know and trust, came alive on it. I sketched Him as I'd seen Him walking the silver path—in profile, features indistinct, yet suggesting gentle strength. I wanted whoever looked at it to recognize Him, yet to realize at the same time the inability of any paintbrush to express His beauty and majesty.

The storm blew itself out as I sketched. The morning broke gray and sullen, and still I sketched, my fingers growing weary in the process.

At last I was satisfied. The Shepherd told His story of love and power; His care held creation in His control. And that included my own little world.

I stood up, stiff and cold. Tomorrow—no today—I would begin selecting my colors—blue-green for His robe, brown for His hair, and far in the distance the sullen, gray, restless ocean waters.

14 / Secret of the Sun

I wakened to the gentle sound of rain and water gurgling in the gutters. Even though the wind had slowed, raindrops splattered at intervals against the windowpanes.

Rain without the sound of wind was soothing. I smiled and pressed deeper inside my blanket nest, picturing other rains. For a moment I was a little girl following the trail of a rain-created stream. I watched a leaf being pushed by the tiny current, raced along the muddy bank, imagining myself perched on that diminutive leaf raft.

I sat up. Christmas was almost here! Even though I had little money to spend, I could do a collection of miniature elf characters as gifts. Using colored pencils, I could capture them in simple lines, mount them on colored construction paper.

Eagerness propelled me out of bed. Deep gray clouds hung heavy behind the sluicing rain blurring the window. But I was eager to be away, to wander through rain-sodden woods in search of inspiration for my sketches.

I'll do a little girl elf for Miss Lavender, I decided. *She'll sit on a pink-tinted mushroom and comb her hair.* And Tiffany would delight in an elf pilot playing the part of a brave captain on a leaf vessel, intent on propelling his small family downstream.

Melissa, I pictured her delight in an elf man swinging from a mossy limb, Darryl enjoying one in a futile attempt to crack a filbert, overwhelmed by a huge hammer.

My imagination ran further. Would Alan enjoy one? He'd loved my clapping hands, the paths of the sea. Would he like something with a whimsical touch, or would he think me foolish and forward?

No. Real interest had gleamed in his eyes when he had

seen my other woodland elves. A sadness rose in me as I realized how little I really knew him, and I had a longing to capture something special, just for him.

After I finished the breakfast clean-up, I donned Miss Lavender's plastic raincoat. She worried aloud, "You'll catch your death of cold if you get wet," and disappeared to rummage in a closet for a pair of rubber boots.

She held them up in triumph, insisting I put them on. I took them reluctantly, disliking their stiff appearance.

But outside with Sea Biscuit beside me, I was glad I had them on. Rain still fell. Every vestige of white had been wiped away and mud lurked everywhere. Sheets of water glistened on the sidewalks, wind gusts caught the thick heavy branches of the evergreens, raining great torrents on my head when I ventured too close.

I stopped beside the creek that ran through the town. Always before it had been small and unobtrusive. Now it gushed swirling brown, debris-filled water, its current thrusting leaves and branches seaward.

A hand touched my arm. I turned. Tiffany, her brown eyes dancing beneath her red hood, laughed up at me.

"So you like it too!" she cried.

We smiled, glad for the other's presence. Our arms looped together and we took off without further words, following the newly awakened stream until we reached the sea.

The heavy rain stirred something inside both of us—a spirit of adventure, excitement in a changed world. The swollen stream shoved leaves, sticks and pop cans headlong into the roaring ocean.

Tiffany put it into neat tidy words as we watched the stream meet the swelling waves. "It's a day for adventure!" she cried. "I think this rain will bring us something unforgettable!"

She whirled to face me. "Colleen, do you think Miss Lavender would let me read her sister's diary? I'd love to find the necklace she wrote about!"

I gave her a quick hug. "You could always ask," I said. I gentled my voice, "But, Tiffany, I don't think you ought to. At least right now. That diary has too many memories, too many hurts stored up inside now. Maybe later.—''

I hated the disappointment that rolled up in Tiffany's eyes. But it left quickly as Sea Biscuit drew close, holding a great stick in his mouth. Tiffany drew it out and tossed it toward the water. Sea Biscuit raced after it. He picked it up and galloped back to her. It seemed as if Sea Biscuit knew that Tiffany needed a distraction right then.

That evening Miss Lavender and I watched the television news. I leaned forward as the newscaster warned of hazardous driving conditions on many of the coastal highways. A large landslide covered the road to the north. To the south a multi-car pile-up had resulted from poor visibility and slick roads.

Miss Lavender shook her head. ''What an unusual year we're having—the October storm, snow, now this.''

I peered out the window, more aware than ever of the pounding rain. ''If this keeps up there'll be flooding, not just here but all over.'' I worried.

The next day the rain continued. The newscasts still warned of floods, possible landslides and hazardous weather conditions. I spent the morning at the kitchen table, colored pencils and paper spread in front of me, marveling at the little elf creatures coming alive from my sketches.

That afternoon I went up the stairs to my studio and tried to visualize the painting that had become vivid in my imagination the night the storm had raged. I selected a canvas and sat down, examining it carefully, seeing the lines that would create the gabled house, the Shepherd, the wind-tossed trees.

A knock sounded on the door. I leapt to my feet, startled. ''Who is it?''

''Alan. May I come in?''

My heart dropped. I hoped he hadn't seen my elf collection still scattered on the kitchen table, especially the elf sailor suspended on a wide-spread sail, challenging an ocean wave. I'd done that one for him.

"Of course," I said, opening the door wide.

"I should have called," he apologized, "but I was jogging through."

I smiled, noting the mud splats that freckled his bright blue jogging suit. I felt unexpectedly warmed because he was comfortable dropping in, casual clothes, mud and all.

He grinned at me. "Care to jog down to the Oyster Shoppe? We could have a bowl of oyster stew, or a Coke. Or would that be interrupting?" he gestured at the empty canvas, the paints laid out in gallant, untouched array.

"I haven't really begun," I said. "I'm still in the planning stage."

"Tell me about it."

"Later. While you're waiting you can help me decide something." I picked up the clapping hands and set it beside the silver paths. "I've been wondering which one to send to the folks."

Alan's attention centered on the silver paths. "Now I see what you *saw* that day," he said softly.

"Yes. Which would you send if you were me?"

Alan stepped back, scrutinizing them carefully. The crinkle deepened between his brows.

I slipped from the room and ran up to my own. I took only a moment to change into a dark blue sweatshirt and tie a matching bandanna over my blond hair.

Alan stood with his legs braced apart, his arms folded. I looked at him uncertainly.

"I've almost decided on the clapping hands," I said tentatively, testing his reaction. "Do you think they'll like it?"

"I suspect they'll like *anything* you do." His hand motioned to the silver paths tracing the waves. "But I think they'd like that best."

"Why?" I demanded.

He turned from the painting and looked full at me. I sensed he saw beyond my dark blue sweatshirt, my upturned nose and blue eyes. I felt he saw my heart, which tripped treacherously.

"The silver paths would give them hope, Colleen." I watched him search for words. "It would give them hope that one day—one day one of those paths would lead you home to them."

Frustration bordering on anger spurted inside me, but I kept it under control. "You think I'm still running!"

"Yes." He turned to me, gripping my arm. "Colleen, there are things in your past you need to come to grips with. Families are so important." A darkness shadowed his eyes. He drew his brows together and I saw trouble surface in his hazel eyes.

"Colleen, I don't talk about it much, but a family is something I've missed all my life." He sat down on the arm of the chair I had recently vacated. One hand came up and he leaned forward, shading his eyes.

"My parents were killed in an airplane crash when I was five years old. My grandfather was the only living relative, and he didn't want me."

His hand dropped to his lap. He lifted his head. "He wrote me a few days ago, Colleen. He's spending Christmas with friends in Salem. He wants to see me."

"And you're going—just like that?"

"Yes. Even though I hardly know him, I want to try to build some kind of relationship."

"But when you were growing up, did he never—"

Alan's hand moved restlessly along his knee. "I stayed with several foster families. One was especially kind. The others . . ." He shook his head. "Granddad wrote sometimes. And he sent me presents on my birthday. I remember the time he gave me an electric train set.

"Last year he stopped by the seminary. We went out to lunch. It was the first time I'd seen him face to face. Colleen, he seemed unhappy, shrunken, not at all the vital man I'd been imagining all my growing up years. He's part of the reason I'm here."

"What does he have to do with 'here'?"

"Years before he set up his business in the Midwest, he'd spent a summer in this little town. He told me it was the happiest time of his life, that he'd left something beautiful and precious here. I guess he'd spent hours exploring on these beaches."

"I thought you came because of your friendship with Jack," I protested. "That's what Jack said."

"That's true enough. We'd known each other from school, and when I found out he was here," he waved his hand airily, "it was an open door to renew old friendships, for ministry, to spend some time where the only family member I have has left some important memories. I thank God for it."

Alan stood abruptly, his wide smile clearing away the past. He reached for my hand. "Let's go!" he exclaimed. Mike's Oyster Shoppe is telling me his oyster stew is steaming hot, just waiting."

I thought about Alan's grandfather that night as Tiffany and I, on impulse, took off for the beach. I'd asked her to spend the night with me, but I almost wished I hadn't. Her restlessness dominated the house. She wandered from room to room, examining the Kewpies downstairs, prowling around the kitchen; then upstairs, looking at my paintings.

Perhaps it was the day's rain that stirred something inside her, perhaps it was the time we'd spent together caught up in the spirit of the swollen creek, the roaring sea driving its restless waves that infected her, eventually driving us outside.

We wandered far up the beach. The rain had stopped its relentless pounding, leaving a harsh wind blowing clouds across the sky. I caught my breath as a star peeked out from behind ragged cloud drapery, almost seeming to pin it back so the moon, huge and full, could rest there in all its glory.

"The moonpath!" Tiffany exclaimed. "See! It's there across the wet sand!"

"I know!" I cried. "I've seen it before!"

"Follow the moonpath," Tiffany exulted, "it leads to the sun. Oh, Colleen, if only I could run on it!"

We ran toward it, but it moved before us, an elusive

path we could never quite find. "It's like a rainbow, Tiffany," I said regretfully, "always just ahead."

It saddened us, stifling our restlessness. We turned homeward.

I sniffed appreciatively as I opened the door. The aroma of burning logs and polished wood made fragrant by the passing years comforted me. We removed our water-soaked tennis shoes in the living room. Afterward we went upstairs and donned warm flannel nightwear and robes.

"Let's have hot chocolate before we go to bed," I suggested.

Tiffany didn't answer. She stood at the window staring down at the rain-soaked garden. "The roses this side of the sundial!" she exclaimed. "They're under water."

Stepping behind her and leaning over her shoulder, I saw a slender glimmering expanse of moonlight tucked between the house and the sundial. The hedge billowed black against the sky. The tips of the rose bushes moved softly, trapping their reflections in the shining otherworld of moonlight, shadows and gently moving water.

A low cry escaped my lips. "The stream's overflowed into the garden!"

Tiffany leaned to one side and we stood together, staring out at the water reflecting the light of the scattered stars, the full moon making a silver path across the faintly rippling water.

Tiffany's awed words echoed my thoughts, "The moon-path—it leads to the sun . . ."

". . . dial," I whispered. "Oh, Tiffany, do you suppose?" Then, "The design inside the sampler, the one I didn't understand!"

My hands trembled as I removed the map from the diary where I had placed it.

We spread it out before the window and looked out. Instead of a crazy design of unexplained circles and squares, I saw the orderly outlines of the hedges, a pond where roses now grew. The circle beyond that was the sundial.

"We need to show this to Miss Lavender," I exclaimed,

"and find out if there used to be a pond there!"

"I knew it!" Tiffany screeched. "Oh, I told you this rain would bring adventure! I could feel it in my bones!"

She picked up the map and we rushed downstairs, Tiffany's excited chant, "Follow the moonpath, just follow the moonpath," keeping pace with us. She burst ahead of me into Miss Lavender's bedroom, flipping on the light switch.

Miss Lavender sat up, her silver hair a fluffy aura around her startled face, her eyes squinting in the sudden lamplight. "What is it?" she cried. "Is something wrong?"

Chagrin that we'd been so thoughtless tangled my tongue. "I'm—we're so sorry, Miss Lavender. It's just that—"

"We followed the moonpath!" Tiffany cried. "We're going to find the treasure."

"What treasure? What moonpath? What *are* you two talking about?" Miss Lavender demanded. She swung her feet over the edge of the bed, pressed her hand over her eyes.

"The map! The pond!" Tiffany explained. In her excitement she bounced down beside her on the bed. "Oh, Miss Lavender, you've got to come and see. You must!"

Miss Lavender looked up at me, bewilderment clouding her eyes. "Colleen?"

"It's the map inside the sampler," I said. "And the light from the moon. You'll have to come upstairs."

"If you say so," she said as she shook her head, folded back her blankets, and followed us out of the room.

I turned to her. "We shouldn't have barged in like this. We're sorry."

"It's all right. If you'd just explain."

"Was there once a pond in the garden. Because if there was—"

"But of course there was. Didn't I tell you? I kept it for years. Then, about ten years ago the upkeep got to be too much for me, so I had to drain the water. Then a neighbor asked if he could haul away the shell."

She sighed heavily. "I loved that pond—hated to see it

go—but one can't hang onto the past forever. I planted roses but it was never the same.''

"I knew it," Tiffany said. "Oh, I knew it."

We hurried up the stairs and we gathered at the window, looking out at the still night. The moon was still shining on the pond, sketching a path across gleaming waters. The sundial picked up its subdued glory, its outlines dimly glowing in the moon's path.

Tiffany laid the open map on the window ledge. Miss Lavender looked at it a long time, then at the moon's reflection riding on the face of the waters. She said only one thing: " 'The path of the just is a shining light that shineth more and more unto the perfect day.' Tomorrow we'll follow that path and discover the secret of the sun.''

15 / The Moon Pendant

Early the next morning we began digging in the garden.

"Do you suppose Amelia buried the pendant under the sundial?" Tiffany asked. She whirled Miss Lavender's shovel in the air while her nimble feet did a sloppy pirouette in the muddy garden.

"Careful of that shovel, young lady." Miss Lavender ducked her head, covering her eyes in mock consternation. "After all, there's no hurry—not if whatever's there has been there for fifty years." Her words sailed past Tiffany.

Tiffany galloped forward, stumbling against the mossy sundial. She caught her balance, panting in anticipation.

"Oh, I'm sure it's here!" she gasped. "It has to be."

I examined the old sundial. The rain had turned the moss embedded in the numbers to a dark rich green that felt soft and moist to my exploring fingertips.

"Let's see if there's any possibility of an opening somewhere first," I said. I shoved against the stiff unyielding center post, then traced the moss-covered numerals. *"Follow the moonpath,"* Amelia had written. *"It leads to the sun."*

"The moon travels clockwise," I murmured, trying to put the puzzle together. "The sun rises in the morning."

Sudden excitement caught in Miss Lavender's cool voice. "It was summertime—the moon could have set before the dawn."

My fingers moved from the four to the six. "These are the early hours. Let's dig under here."

Tiffany shoved the shovel at an angle into the water saturated earth beneath the ancient concrete base. The ground slurped in irritation. With Tiffany's next eager shove, we heard a click. Miss Lavender and I stared at each other.

"It's there! It's got to be!" Tiffany shouted. She dropped to her knees on the sodden ground and pushed both hands into the opening.

"Oh, rats!" She ejaculated. Her muddy hands came out empty and she seized the shovel.

"Be careful," I entreated, slowing the shovel action with a firm grip on the handle.

We both felt the solid clunk against the blade. "Go slowly, Tiffany," I pleaded. "We don't want to damage it, whatever we do."

"Yes, please . . ." Miss Lavender added. "Do be careful."

Together we slid the shovel back out. This time I knelt beside her, shoving my hands where the shovel blade had been. My fingers made immediate contact with a hard unyielding substance.

"It feels like metal—a box."

The mud squiggled around my fingers but I wouldn't let go. I curled my fingers around the object and pulled hard. The mud released its grip and I fell backward, holding the small, mud-encrusted box triumphantly high.

"Oh, Colleen!" Miss Lavender cried. "It looks like it might be the real thing. Do you suppose?"

"But of course!" Tiffany exclaimed. She pushed close, one hand reaching out to touch the mystery box.

"It's old," I observed, turning the box in my hand. "I see rust mixed with the mud. And it's rough—pitted with age."

"But how will we open it?" Tiffany wondered.

I smeared the mud inquisitively. "There's a latch on the side. I can feel it. Let's take it inside and clean it off. Then we'll know what we have."

I stood, my muddy jeans clinging uncomfortably. Miss Lavender led the way to the house, her silver head held expectantly high. I wondered what she was feeling.

We gathered around the kitchen sink and let cold water rush away the orange-stained mud. We could see that it was made of heavy metal, roughened by time.

I pried the latch, and then the lid. Hinges squeaked in rusty protest. Three heads bent close as the lid lifted to reveal a smaller metal box, not as pitted or rusty.

"I see the keyhole," I said. "If we only had the key—"

"Maybe we could break it open with an axe," Tiffany affirmed.

I shook my head, releasing a jet of water into the tiny hole with the spray nozzle attached to the sink. Tiffany's hand hovered over the box. I placed it in her palm. "You're holding a piece of yesterday in your hand, Tiffany. Treat it gently." I turned to Miss Lavender. "Is the box familiar at all?"

Miss Lavender shook her head. "I've never seen it before." An odd speculative look gathered in her gray eyes. I saw far-off memories stir and I held my breath. Would she share?

Disappointment surged through me as she turned and walked out of the kitchen. "Sometimes she makes me so mad!" I spluttered. "She's so secretive—so private."

But Tiffany was gentler in her judgment. "It's her past," she said. "I expect it colors one's present."

"And one's future," I mused. "I'm sorry, Tiffany. I shouldn't have—" I pulled a paper towel from the holder and laid it on the counter. "Put the box here."

Tiffany set the box on the towel and we stepped back. My imagination rushed inside me. Was there really something beautiful tucked safely away after so many years? It didn't seem likely.

Or did it? I whirled around at Miss Lavender's soft step. A quiet glow radiated from her face. She dropped something into Tiffany's palm.

Tiffany's excited squeal filled the kitchen. "A key!" she cried. "Do you think it'll fit? Where did you find it?"

"To answer your first question—I don't know whether it will or not. And the second—Amelia gave it to me years ago, several months before she died. I'd forgotten that she'd said I was to guard it carefully, follow the moonpath. And something about a message.''

She shook her silver head. "I don't pretend to understand what she meant. I didn't then and I don't now—but the key just might fit. Go ahead. Open it.''

Tiffany's fingers fumbled, then steadied. I watched the deep scowl of concentration furrow her forehead, the squint lines crowd around her eyes. Then a smile like a rainbow after rain broke across her face.

"It's turning!''

Miss Lavender and I leaned forward. The lid opened slowly, stiff with disuse.

A star-flecked moon nestled against a black velvet cloth, untouched by the years. A soft gasp slid from Miss Lavender's lips.

Tiffany's finger reached out, touching the tiny star glints reflecting off the round moon-shaped pendant. "It's beautiful,'' she breathed. Gently, almost reverently, her slender fingers began untangling the delicate silver chain suspended from the pendant.

"It's so delicate,'' Miss Lavender marveled. "I've never seen it before. I wonder what Amelia meant. A message.—''

"It might come,'' Tiffany encouraged as she laid it gently in her hand. "Maybe later you'll remember.''

But Miss Lavender only shook her head sadly. "Not at my age, dear. Not at my age.''

"But you never know,'' Tiffany insisted. "Didn't you just now remember the key? Couldn't something else trigger another memory later?''

Miss Lavender didn't appear to be listening. "Why would he give her such an expensive gift?'' she mused. "Do you suppose he really loved her—after all?''

I could only slip an arm around her. "I don't know. But now that we've found the pendant she talked about, who knows, maybe we can find Lawrence's family and return it to them.''

Tiffany handed the necklace to Miss Lavender. "Thank

you," she said. "It means a lot to me to be in on Amelia's secret."

I knew what she meant. Somehow the pendant had drawn Miss Lavender, Tiffany and me closer together. I looked out the window. The clouds had lost their rosy flush but they were still beautiful, huddling together like fluffy sheep touched with sunlight. The day stretched before us, as fresh and untouched as whitened sand at low tide, full of invitation and promise.

A tiny piece of that promise was realized late that afternoon. I had spent the morning painting in the finishing touches to the silver paths and was pleased. Then I'd striven to capture the force of the wind in my storm painting. No matter how I tried, the trees failed to twist, the wind to scream its rage at the shielding Shepherd.

I welcomed the telephone's shrill demand funneling up the stairs. I put my brush down and ran to answer it. Even Pete would be a diversion. But it wasn't Pete.

Alan went straight to the subject he wanted to talk about. "The Christmas party at church, Colleen," he said. "I'd be pleased if you'd go with me . . ." he paused. "If you're still in town."

Guilt swept in on me. "You mean if I don't go home?" I asked.

"Yes. Are you going, Colleen?"

The turbulence I'd been trying so hard to capture in my storm painting rolled up inside me. For a moment I almost lashed out at him. Then the picture of the Good Shepherd swept into my mind. A stillness that had nothing to do with me, my family, or Alan or Pete welled up inside.

"Go in peace. Your faith has made you whole." Jesus had said that to a woman who washed His feet with her tears and wiped them with her hair. He promised her peace.

"Colleen, are you there?"

"Yes, of course. I'd like to go with you to the party, Alan. Is it formal, informal? What shall I wear?"

Afterward I wondered at my reaction. But it didn't matter. I knew then what my subject for my personal quiet time with the Lord needed to be: peace, His peace—the kind that goes beyond mere human understanding.

The next few days rushed by. The high water and relentless rain receded into dense foggy mornings and dark early evenings that cried out for Christmas lights and laughter. Pete brought us a tree and I spent hours arranging and rearranging Miss Lavender's old-fashioned hand-painted balls and fragile angels. Then I decorated her living room with fresh cedar and bright holly and carefully selected tall graceful tapers for the centerpiece in the middle of the dining room table.

The holiday busyness almost pushed aside the excitement we'd felt over the discovery of Amelia's pendant. But not quite. After our initial growing together in sharing that special moment, something had changed. Miss Lavender had suddenly withdrawn, grown remote. When I'd mentioned something about taking steps to locate Lawrence Redgate's family, she'd said, "Let it rest, Colleen, let it rest. Maybe after the holidays."

"Is it because she's missing those who've gone before?" I asked the Christmas angels banded at the top of the tree. "Or is she still haunted by regrets from the past?"

The angels didn't answer. But I was sure the soft wind unexpectedly stealing around the corner of the house whispered, *Peace I give unto you. My peace.*

That evening Pete drove down from Garibaldi for an evening in Miss Lavender's kitchen. Together we cluttered the counters and table with colored frosting and brown fudge smudges.

"It's little things like candlelight and silver paper that make Christmas special," I said. I gestured around the disorderly kitchen. "And candy, cookies . . ."

Pete looked up from the rosy-cheeked snowman cookie he was trying to decorate. "But a snowman *should* have white cheeks, shouldn't he?"

"Not this one," I said recklessly. "Let's pretend someone pushed two bright apples into his cheeks to give him a healthy glow.''

"Either that, or make him into a Santa Claus—"

I sat down opposite him and scrutinized the snowman. "Pete, I like him.''

Pete laid his knife on the table and leaned forward, grasping my hand. "Colleen,'' he said, urgency making his voice almost harsh. "I have to talk to you.''

I drew back. "We're talking now.''

"No, we're not. We're only talking trivia. Colleen, I have to know. Do you have any feeling at all for me besides friendship?''

"Pete!'' I cried. "Don't you understand? The feeling I have for you goes back to when you found me—a frightened, rebellious girl. You reached out to me then and—and I loved you for it—will always love you.''

"That's not enough, Colleen.'' His words were filled with longing, "Not anymore.''

"Isn't it? Pete, you need to think things through. Remember your suggestion that I live with your sister—become polished and proper? That isn't me! It won't ever be! I'd be miserable living in town, becoming a career girl, a lady of fashion. Except for my painting, I'm a plain person. I like simple things like beaches, and elves, and Christmas candy.''

"And little white churches?'' The bitterness in his voice made me wince.

"And families.'' I thrust my chin forward courageously. "I'm beginning to see how important they are. Pete, you need to find someone else. I'm not the girl you have pictured in your heart. *That* girl doesn't exist.''

Pete dropped my hand and stood abruptly. "Colleen—"

"I know you mean well, that you care. But you've already done enough for me—maybe too much. And, Pete— I care. I really do.''

"So—the answer is no.'' The hurt finality in his voice bruised me. His dark blue stricken eyes gave me one long last look before he got up and turned to the door. "Someday, perhaps, I'll thank you."

Then he was gone, his footsteps echoing hollowly against the porch boards. The sound of his motor reverberated across the lawn, through the walls, and into my heart.

The day of the Christmas party dawned sullen and cold with frozen fog furring the tree branches. All day I waited for the sun to break through, but it never did. Toward evening I went upstairs and sat looking out my window.

Pete's abrupt departure from my life smarted. I'd tried hard not to think by submerging myself in activity. The feeling of loss remained. I didn't want Pete's romance, but I did want his friendship.

After a while I laid out the flame red dress I'd finished several days before. I touched the orange red material, marveling at how the moment I'd seen the material in the store, I'd been able to visualize just what it would look like.

The next day I'd finished the gifts for my family and sent them off in the mail, except for a painting to my parents. I was still unsure of which to send, and wanted time to make sure it was exactly right. I'd pushed aside my twinge of guilt as the postman stepped into the back, carrying my package. Mailing them had made me feel more alone then ever.

As soon as I had returned home I'd distracted myself by cutting and sewing. The dress emerged like a butterfly from a cocoon. It took shape before my eyes, a flaming creation that brought clear blue lights into my eyes I hadn't known they'd possessed. My blond hair shone a red gold, bringing translucent glow to my skin.

I took a long leisurely shower, applied makeup, then slipped the dress over my head. After I brushed my hair till it gleamed, I turned in front of the mirror, noting the gold accentuated against the flaming dress. *Like burning coals in the fireplace.*

I picked up my purse and ran down the stairs. Miss Lavender sat with her chair drawn close to the fire, a lacy shawl draped over her legs. I stopped, struck by the lonely picture she portrayed. Was she seeing the low burning flames—or memories?

"Miss Lavender!" I went to her and knelt beside her, burying my face against the warm fuzzy material of her shawl.

"Why, child," she murmured. "What is it?"

I lifted my face to hers. "You looked so alone," I faltered. "I—I don't need to go out."

A smile slid across her faded features. "Yes, you do, Miss Marigold. Yes, you do." One of her hands moved gently over my hair. "Stand up, Colleen. That dress—is that the one you made?"

I nodded. "It does something, doesn't it?"

She gestured across the room. "Walk over there, would you? I want to get the effect."

I obeyed. Feeling slightly foolish, I did a model half turn—then lifted my hands, careening in a circle.

Miss Lavender nodded. "It's right, just right, but that neck needs something. Wait here—" She stood up and walked toward her room. At the door she turned and smiled. "Don't go now."

"I won't," I assured her. I knelt in front of the Christmas tree, and began to rearrange the Kewpies I'd placed beneath it. "Enjoying the good evergreen smell?" I asked their eternally smiling faces.

I read the answer in their bright round black eyes. All it took was imagination to know they were enjoying the lights and fragrance of Christmas.

"Now, if you'll just sit still a moment." I jumped at the sound of Miss Lavender's voice. "And close your eyes."

Something light and fragile settled around my neck. My eyes flew open. "Amelia's pendant!" I cried. "Oh, Miss Lavender, I can't wear that! It's too precious to you, to your sister!"

I whirled to face her. Her reply was a hand mirror thrust in front of my face. I stared at the girl, looking back at me— vibrant, alive, yet somehow vulnerable and unsure.

My eyes dropped to the moon pendant nestled in the

hollow of my throat. My hand reached up and touched it gently. "It's so beautiful," I faltered, "too beautiful for me."

"No, Colleen. You're a lovely girl. Even though I haven't let Amelia's pendant out of my room since it returned, I want you to wear it tonight—for Alan—for me. But most of all for you.

"You see, my dear, I love you. You're the daughter—well, perhaps the granddaughter—I never had and always wanted."

The question I'd wondered so long, stumbled to my lips. "But why? If you always wanted a family, why did you never marry?"

I regretted my question as soon as I'd uttered it, hating the look of dark regret surfacing in her gray eyes. "Miss Lavender . . ."

She reached for the mirror in my hand. A sad smile touched her lips as she studied her reflection. "I was so busy running from God—from one man to the other—that by the time I really knew what I wanted, it was too late." She handed the mirror back to me. "Don't make the same mistake I did, my dear. I know you won't." She turned and went back to her room.

I sat there a long time staring after her. I only stirred when the doorbell rang.

16 / Rainbow Wings

Alan stood on the porch, framed against the night sky. Behind him a clear moon rode high, highlighting a skiff of tattered clouds. His lips parted, then closed.

I squirmed uncomfortably beneath his gaze. "The fog," I said, searching for thoughts, ideas, anything to distract myself from the admiration I saw in his eyes.

"It's been around us like a mantel all day," I chattered. "Odd it should wait 'til darkness to lift. Come inside. I'll get my coat."

He stepped behind me into the warm lamplit room. "I hate to do this," he apologized. "That pendant, your dress . . ." Without ceremony he thrust a plain paper bag into my arms. "Would you be willing to wear this for part of the evening?"

I peered into the open bag, then drew out a swath of dark midnight blue material. I shook it out and held the long shapeless dress beneath my chin. "What is it?" I asked, lifting my puzzled gaze to his penetrating look.

"Al and Lucy can't come tonight. They were part of a surprise."

My fingers caressed the soft cloth. "Surprise?"

"A pageant. Tonight for the party. It's to be in Wilhelm's barn. Nobody knows except those who have a part."

I looked down at the long dress of midnight blue. "And Lucy was to be Mary?"

Alan nodded. "And Al, Joseph. Would you mind too much, Colleen? Being Mary, I mean. Of course we'll miss the party fun in the beginning. But after the pageant—"

"But I won't know what to do," I protested. "Do I need to say anything?"

"No. Just be willing to be Mary. And—if you could

somehow get into Mary's mind. Visualize what she felt, try to experience some of the wonder. That would help it come alive." He reached out his hand and lifted the dark blue gown away from my neck. "I almost hate to have you do it. You look so vibrant—so alive in your dress. And that lovely pendant—is that the one Tiffany told me about?"

"Yes. Gone all those years."

A nostalgic smile softened Alan's face. "Time," he murmured, "so many years. Will you play Mary's part, Colleen? All you have to do is follow my lead, lose yourself in the story."

My chin jerked up. "You're to be Joseph?"

Alan's left brow quirked up. "Does that bother you?"

Flame that matched my dress leaped into my cheeks. "Of course not." I laid the bag in a chair and started to the closet for my coat. "Where do we change? In the barn?"

Alan smiled, his eyes alight as he looked at me. "I knew you'd be like that," he said.

At his words, the barrier twisted around my heart broke and melted in an unexpected rush of tenderness. "Mary," I faltered. "She says something to me. She was so—so available and willing. Not like me."

Impulsively, Alan reached out and touched my hands.

"Colleen," he pleaded, his voice winged with fire yet touched with steel. "You *can* be like that. I see such beauty in you—such sensitivity . . ."

His hands tightened over mine, his tone growing suddenly tender. "You have so much to give others—me."

I looked sharply into his eyes, saw his love shining through like a flame. *No, Alan, no. I'm not like that.*

I stiffened and withdrew my hands. A veil dropped over his face. With mixed emotions, I turned and opened the closet door and put on a soft brown coat. Would I ever understand myself?

The old barn, softened by lantern light and the confusion of voices, drew Alan and me into another world. Shepherds, dark with beards and grease paint, huddled together in a corner singing. "This, this, is Christ the King. The babe, the son of Mary . . ."

A young wise man, full of joy and high spirits, flung himself toward them, his purple robe floating about him, as he lifted his voice to join the shepherds.

Alan gestured to a stall on the right, far back from the door. "The girls are dressing there."

I stood tightly clutching my paper bag. "Your beard," I said impulsively. "You shouldn't have shaved it off."

Alan rubbed his chin ruefully. "I miss it too," he said. "Someday—" He changed the subject abruptly. "Now scat. We're already late."

The stall door slid open and an angel with tall rainbow wings stood before us. "Do you like my costume?"

She whirled before me. I marveled at the radiance of the shining blue folds that picked up the irridescent colors in the wings.

"It's different from the way I imagine angels," I said, "but somehow so right."

The other six angels gathered around me and I saw that each gown was a different color of the spectrum. When they stood together they would create a rainbow. I pulled out the midnight blue dress.

"Lucy couldn't come," I said. "Alan asked me to be Mary."

Jill, her mouth filled with safety pins, was busy anchoring a pair of wings on the smallest angel. "I'll help you in a minute, Colleen—if you need help."

I laid my coat over the door and slid the dress over my head. "I'll need a safety pin to anchor the headpiece," I said as I reached into the bag for the long swath of dove gray material.

"You'll need to cover your hair," Jill said. "Mary's was dark brown, not blond." She leaned forward, helping me adjust the folds around my shoulders, tuck in the stray bits of blond hair that pushed rebelliously around its edges.

We walked out together. Alan waited for me by the door. I smiled as he held out his hand. I took it without self-consciousness, a tiny something inside me thrilling at its naturalness.

"You look the way I imagine Joseph," I confided. "Your beard suits you."

He looked at me critically. "Your hair—what have you done with it?"

"They said it was the wrong color."

"Nonsense." He pulled me outside the barn door and stopped. I felt a hot flush rise in my cheeks as he pulled several tendrils free from the mantel. "There, that's better. Now for what you're to do: after everyone's gathered, we're to go to the house and seek entrance, but there won't be any room. We'll wait on the screen porch in the back."

We walked slowly toward the house, still hand in hand. Overhead the stars and moon danced with creation joy. Low on the horizon rested the evening star. *Probably Venus,* I thought. *No, this is a night of miracles . . . the star of Bethlehem.*

We stood together in the porch darkness, waiting for our cue. Suddenly there was a soft whisper, "They're ready."

Alan's fist pounded the door. "Open up!" he shouted. We need a room!"

The door quickly opened. "If it's a room you're looking for, you'll have to look elsewhere!" Pastor Jack exclaimed.

A hush fell over the holiday crowd. I blinked in the light. My shoulders drooped. Alan's hand squeezed mine.

"Please, sir," he said firmly, "we've come far. The roads have been long and my wife is about to have a baby."

"Then you shouldn't have been so foolish to undertake such a journey," a voice from the back of the room called.

"I'm sorry," Pastor Jack apologized. He stood before us, tall and distinguished in his suit of medium blue. "It's just that we're—well—we're right in the middle of a party and . . . You could try the house next door, though."

Joseph looked down at me. I felt my lips quiver and covered them with my hand. "I'm sorry, Mary," he said. "I shouldn't have brought you so far from home." He touched the back of my head and I felt his tenderness.

"I'm all right," I reassured. "We had no choice."

Joseph looked hard at Pastor Jack. "Please," he entreated, "could we have access to one of your rooms? The need is great."

"I'm sorry," he said—"But wait. There's a barn in back. You could stay there. You'd be quite comfortable."

"But—you don't understand!"

"It's all right, Joseph," I said. "It will be quiet there. Come."

Joseph's arm slid around me. We turned away. And it was as though we stepped into the past together. We crossed the field and I suddenly felt desolate and alone—far from home.

The shepherds, wise men and angels had disappeared and the barn's emptiness brooded around us. I sank to my knees beside the manger, suddenly overwhelmed with the greatness of my role.

Alan gathered my heart close to him and to God as he knelt beside me, bowed his head and prayed, "Lord, direct us tonight. Let us feel your glory. Let us show to all who come the meaning of your coming."

An angel slipped softly up to me, holding Joe and Carrie's infant son swatched in a soft white blanket, folded round and round.

Tears stung my eyes as I held him close to my heart. *And the Word was made flesh and dwelt among us. And we beheld his glory.*

I paid little attention as the barn filled with guests. My thoughts were held captive by the tiny hand that clung to mine, the soft hair that curled off the baby's forehead.

A spirit of prayer surged around me as the mighty words of "O Come, All Ye Faithful" spilled over me. Then an unseen voice poured forth the love of "Unto Us a Son Is Given."

The words "And she brought forth her first born son and laid him in the manger" pulsated with new meaning. I snuggled the infant into the hay Joseph placed there for him and pulled his blanket close around him.

Never a night like this, I thought, *or ever a story more beautifully told.*

The shepherds came—great, hulking, unsure country folk, clad in the dun colors of the earth. They knelt beside the manger and I smiled at them, noticing for the first time the sheep in the pen behind them.

Another shepherd, this one burly and demanding, charged up to the manger. "Let us see the baby!" he shouted. "We've seen an angel." The voice softened as he knelt in front of the baby: "The Holy One, the promised Son of God."

Angels descended from the loft and grouped around the manger with reverent faces and outstretched hands, making a promise arching over us.

Wise men came and laid their gifts before him. Their voices lifted in song, "O Holy Night."

Light glistened off the angel's rainbow wings. Then one of them knelt and blew out the lantern. A holy hush wrapped us in its caress as we all knelt and sang *"Silent Night, Holy Night"* in the soft darkness.

The story was told. The guests surged outside, exclaiming and talking. A small boy darted forward. He reached into the manger and clutched at the infant hand. "He's real!" he shouted. "He's real!" Then he was out the barn door, his vibrant moving body expressing his joy that Jesus was born.

Somehow I didn't want to go back to the house. The story had been too much a part of me. Feelings too reverent and real to sully with casual merrymaking burned inside me.

Alan understood when I tried to explain. "But I need to be there, Colleen," he said gently. "They're my people. And they've worked hard. They need me to share their triumph."

A momentary flash of resentment coursed through me. *Must others needs always come before one's own?*

Then the spirit of the woman I'd been playing stirred inside me. Mary knew what it was to put the needs of a dying world ahead of her own.

It seemed unreal to slip off my coat and move gaily

among the crowds in my red Christmas dress. But I did it. I even found myself enjoying the admiration expressed for my part in the play.

I was sipping festive holiday punch, testing the delicate red—and—green sugared cookie Alan brought me when a hand touched my shoulder. "Colleen!"

I whirled around. "Pete! I didn't know you were here."

Pete's dark blue eyes searched mine. "I was in the barn," he said softly. "You played the part of Mary with beauty and feeling. I'll never forget it."

"Thank you. I—"

Jill, the tall angel whose mouth had held safety pins minutes before, now pouted adorably, putting her hand on Pete's shoulder. "Pete, you promised."

Oh, Pete, my heart cried, *are you trying to make me jealous or is this some wonderful new thing? Are you taking my words to heart about finding someone who's more like you want me to be?*

Even as I watched, Pete looked at Jill. Half of the room separated us but I recognized the interest in his eyes. Only a short while before it had reached out to me.

They moved away. Jill's long red hair swung almost to her waist, contrasting with the metallic purple and green diagonal stripe in her dress. Pete's hand touched the small of her back.

My hand stole to the hollow in my throat, seeking the comfort of the moon pendant. My heart plunged into my stomach. My neck was bare!

The party swung in festive mood around me as my eyes searched for Alan. He was nowhere to be seen. I set my half-eaten cookie and punch on the table and slipped unnoticed through the crowd.

The night welcomed me. Venus had risen high on the horizon and—I caught my breath—stood directly over the old barn, its lines blurred in the dim light.

Alan found me an hour later, still searching through the hay. "I've looked everywhere for you!" he exclaimed.

He must have read the desolation in my face, for he

dropped to his knees beside the lantern and put his arm across my shoulder. I had the awful impulse to turn to him and sob out my disappointment and loss, but I held back.

"I've lost Amelia's pendant," I said flatly. "I've retraced our steps to the house by lantern light, searched the stall where we dressed—the manger. It's gone."

"Have you checked the house?" Alan asked.

I shook my head, "I thought at first that it probably came loose when I was dressing, so I came here."

Alan reached for my hand. "We'll go back to the house. We'll ask questions, look everywhere. Someone must have seen it."

But no one had. Wise men, shepherds, angels and guests banded together and looked in every possible nook and crannie to no avail.

"I'll search the barn and grounds by daylight," Alan reassured me as we stepped onto the porch. "It has to be somewhere."

"After all those years buried beneath the sundial, lost the first time it's worn," I mourned. "I hate to tell Miss Lavender—dread it."

"It will be easier in the morning," Alan comforted.

But the feeling of night stretching long before me lingered even after we returned home. Alan would soon be leaving . . .

"I did something for you for Christmas," I said shyly. "I'll get it for you now."

I hurried up the stairs and picked up the elf sketch I'd wrapped in silver paper. He took it eagerly, turning it in his hands.

"May I open it now or must I wait?"

"Take it with you," I entreated, "and when you come back—"

I didn't finish my sentence. One of Alan's arms came out and clasped me close. For a moment I felt his strength, his cheek against my hair.

Then he was gone and I went upstairs. I undressed, donned my bathrobe and slipped across the hall. The silver paths in my painting beckoned to me, reminding me of angel wings, moon pendants, the whisper of song and the feel of Alan's arm tight around me . . .

"Shepherd of the Sea," I whispered, "which silver path is mine? What direction does it lead? Home? to Alan? Lord Jesus, you love lost things like me, and sheep and coins. You know where lost things are. You care. Hold tight to Amelia's moon pendant. Help us find it soon."

A lump welled up in my throat and I couldn't say anymore. But I knew He understood. After a while I went to bed, my mind still searching beneath the hay, probing into unlikely corners. And all the while I pictured Alan beside me, clasping my hand.

My dream that night was a single glowing moon pendant that reflected rainbow colors. It hung suspended from a solitary star, shedding to earth a glow of hope.

I think it cast a hue of rainbow light onto a silver path . . .

17 / The Stones Cry Out

I wakened to morning light steaming across the dress I'd carelessly tossed onto the chair the night before. With it came the memory of Amelia's lost pendant.

My stomach plunged. Then the accompanying desolation tangled with hope.

Voices drifted up the stairs and I recognized Alan's deep tones. Had he found the pendant? Was he returning it to Miss Lavender? I shot out of bed, leapt into blue jeans and blouse, whisked a comb through my hair.

I stopped short in the open doorway. Alan and Miss Lavender, the brown head and the silver, were close together, oblivious to my presence, intently examining an unseen object cradled in Alan's hand. I started to exclaim, "The moon pendant!" but the words were never uttered.

"I don't want Colleen to know," I heard Alan say softly.

I stepped backward, fading into the hallway. What was happening? What was it Alan wanted to keep from me? Why were they shutting me out? I turned and stole softly back up the stairs.

My studio welcomed me but my conscience twisted inside as I observed my unfinished painting pushed into the corner. I'd neglected it while I'd dabbled with my elf characters. My storm was still an unrealized vision of a night when panic had been replaced with peace.

Almost of their own volition my hands selected the sea colors I'd previously laid out. I pulled up the old discarded stool I'd brought from the basement and picked up my brush.

There was a knock. "Yes?"

I sat with my brush poised in front of me, my eyes questioning.

Alan entered. "I didn't think you'd be asleep, not with

Amelia's pendant gone.'' He stretched his cupped hand out to me. ''The lost is found,'' he said softly.

''I'm glad,'' I said simply. ''Does—does Miss Lavender know?''

He looked at me searchingly. ''I just talked to her.''

''I know. I heard voices.'' I picked up the moon pendant, dangling it indifferently across my palm. ''Why didn't you give it to her?''

''Because—'' his searching look was suddenly replaced with an impish grin—''I wanted to see your face when you saw it safe and sound.''

Filled with remorse at my childish reaction, I said, ''I'm sorry, Alan. I guess I wanted you to come racing up to show me first of all. I was being childish—but I do thank you. Tell me, where did you find it?''

''Inside the manger, pushed into the corner.''

''Funny—I looked there. I know I did.''

''The light was bad. Besides, some things can be hidden in plain sight. But this was sort of sideways, hidden by hay. Colleen, I'm going away in the morning.''

My eyes flashed to his, startled. ''So soon?''

''Yes. I talked to my grandfather on the phone this morning. I'm going early.''

''Will you still miss Christmas here?'' I asked.

Light flashed in his eyes. He grabbed my hand. ''Colleen, if I really thought—''

''What?'' I breathed.

''That you cared even a tiny bit. Oh, Colleen . . .''

I pulled my hand free and turned to my paintings. ''As you can see I haven't sent the 'silver paths' to Mom and Dad,'' I babbled. ''I was hoping I'd find someone going that direction. Any chance you'll be going as far north as Portland? They're just off the freeway—only a few miles from Tualatin.''

The light in his eyes faded. ''No. Wait—I could too. In fact, I'd like to. I could take an afternoon and drive north.'' He strode over to the silver paths.

His fine long fingers caressed the edge thoughtfully.

When he looked at me again, his eyes were veiled.

I lifted my chin. "You don't need to."

"I know," he said, "but I want to." His hand wandered to the silver path in front of the Shepherd's feet and I wondered what he was thinking.

His next words caught me off guard. "Tell me, Colleen. What message will you send them? Will I be the bearer of good tidings? Or—"

He never finished his question. I turned and whirled from the room.

That night Miss Lavender challenged me with a question of her own. We were dawdling over a late light supper of toast and applesauce when she put down her spoon. "Look at me, Colleen."

I lifted smoky rebellious eyes to hers. "Why?" I asked sullenly.

She touched her cool hand to my hot cheek. "Because you look so miserable, child. What is it? Alan going away?"

"No!" I exclaimed angrily. "It's just that he tries to be my conscience, that's all."

She didn't pursue the subject. "Or could it be you heard us sharing our thoughts over Amelia's moon pendant and you're chafing over it?"

I jumped to my feet. "Miss Lavender! If you and he want to talk together, it's nothing to me!"

"It is if you heard him say he didn't want me to tell you something. Did you, Colleen?"

I sat back down abruptly. My fingers began to toy with the edge of the red and green placemat. "Yes. I did."

Miss Lavender nodded. "I thought as much." She reached out and patted my hand. "It's given you a miserable day."

She stood, pushing back her chair. "I want you to know what we were discussing—at least my part of it. Wait." She left the room and my eyes suddenly smarted with tears.

The tree lights cracked and splintered, leaving me open and vulnerable. *Oh, God, I'm sorry. Forgive me for not following your path. Forgive me. . . .*

I slipped into the living room and stood in front of the tree, looking up into the fragrant evergreen branches, seeing more than angels and beautiful old balls. I remembered instead a manger, a little hand that clung and a star that hung like a pendant suspended from heaven.

Miss Lavender broke into my reverie. "There's something about Amelia's moon pendant you need to know, Colleen," she said.

I turned to face her. She held the pendant out to me and I took it. "When Alan discovered it this morning it was slightly ajar—like so." Her slim white fingers pressed it. Where before there had been only a seam of gold, a tiny crack appeared.

Miss Lavender pried her fingernail inside and lifted. The pendant sprang apart, revealing a small burnished red-gold agate inside.

"But I had no idea!" I gasped. "Nor did Tiffany."

"Nor I. It doesn't look like a locket at all. But that agate hidden inside is precious to me, Colleen. It's—it's a voice from the past," her own lowered. "It says Amelia forgave me, totally and unconditionally. That was why she kept whispering to me to follow the moonpath."

"I don't understand!" I exclaimed. The tiny stone rolled beneath my finger as I tried to pick it up. "What does it mean?"

I tried again to capture the elusive agate, this time lifting it to my palm. "It's no bigger than a seed pearl I saw once," I murmured. "It's hard to visualize a tiny thing like this carrying a great big message of forgiveness."

Miss Lavender smiled. "It's one of those little things Zechariah tells us not to despise. This little agate has a story to tell."

She pulled up a chair and sat down, patting the arm companionably. "Come, listen."

I sat down on the carpet instead and pillowed my head against her knee like a small child. "I don't know how it started," she began. "But as far back as I can remember, little rocks were a special symbol of forgiveness between us.

"Maybe it was because we associated rocks with the sea, and mother always said that when God forgave us, He buried all memory of our sin into its depths. We'd go to the beach and Amelia would shout, 'As far as the east is from the west, so far has He removed our sins from us.' Then I'd answer, 'He buries all our transgressions into the depths of the sea, and remembers them no more.' "

Miss Lavender smiled her silver smile, the one that turned her eyes into the silvery past. "How my tongue loved rolling over that big word—transgressions. I can still remember the goose bumps that rose on my arms. Anyway, I think that's where the association began. Whenever one of us did something to hurt the other, we'd give the other a small rock to ask for forgiveness. Then the one receiving the stone would return it as a promise that nothing would ever be said again about it, that it was forgiven and forgotten the way God did it by burying it in the ocean."

"In the depths of the sea," I murmured. "That's beautiful, Miss Lavender—beautiful."

"Except the last time, Colleen. The very last time. I knew things between us weren't right because of Lawrence. Oh, I never knew or understood then how my foolish flirting had damaged their relationship, but I knew I'd hurt her.

"I gave her a stone, Colleen, this tiny agate, and asked her to forgive me. She never returned it."

I jumped up and laid my cheek against her silken silver hair. "Oh, Miss Lavender!"

Her voice was hardly more then a whisper, a sorrowing whisper like low wind through the woods when the sun has left. "I never knew 'til today that she forgave me completely and unconditionally. All these years I thought she carried unforgiveness to her deathbed. And how it hurt! Oh, I know God forgave me, but I couldn't forgive myself, not completely."

"And now?"

Miss Lavender smiled. "I have peace. I had peace with

Jesus years ago, but now I have peace with Amelia.'' She stood up. ''Did you know peace means wholeness, a restoration of a relationship? That's the real message of Christmas.''

After she had gone to bed, I sat by the Christmas tree for a long time. First I thought about God's peace. Then about Lawrence—Amelia—Miss Lavender.

Somehow that started my thoughts down another track: Alan—Pete—myself—Jill. I moved uncomfortably. Pete had been different at the party.

''I should be glad if he likes Jill,'' I whispered. ''But I'm not—exactly. I think I feel a little bit like Miss Lavender did—jealous, rejected even though I made it very clear I wasn't the person he needed, or even really wanted.

''Why should I feel this way? He's my friend who reached out to me, believed in me when I was filled with turmoil. And Alan. . . ?''

The lights winked on and off, the angels and Kewpies smiled, and suddenly I understood. Peace wasn't dependent on people. It began in the heart and worked out through the eyes and smiles of His people.

Miss Lavender said peace was one of the names of God: *Jehovah Shalom*—God my peace.

That afternoon my storm painting pulled at me. I put down the gaily decorated wrapping paper I was folding and slipped upstairs.

I picked up my brush. I wanted my Shepherd's brown hair to fly around His face, the folds of His blue robe to quiver and come alive in response to the raging wind.

My thoughts winged forward. *I want it to say something about you, Lord Jesus. Something special about Jehovah Shalom, the God of peace in the midst of storm.*

How could I do it? How could I capture the beautiful balance in the force of the wind, the strength of my Savior? How could I translate the peace I was learning into feeling so deep that all who looked at my painting would sense its presence?

My brush moved carefully over the canvas. The brown of His hair . . . The blue of His robe . . .

A knock startled me from my concentration. "Yes?"

Pete opened the door. "I can't stop right now," I said, waving my brush to the chair.

"Perhaps I'd better go," Pete hesitated. "I—"

"No, please stay. I'll stop in a minute." I added darkness to the shadowy folds of the Shepherd's robe, making it dance with new life.

I laid my brush down and leaned back, squinting my eyes. "Am I doing it, Pete? Does it really *say* what I want it to?"

Pete looked at the painting, his handsome features tense, drawn sharp in concentration. "It's not finished yet," I said hesitantly.

"That doesn't matter. Already it speaks to me."

"What does it *say*, Pete?" I asked eagerly. "What do you feel when you look at it?"

"The Lord Jesus Christ—sovereign—in control of every circumstance that can ever touch me. I see His power, Colleen, feel His greatness—His peace."

The barrier surrounding my heart suddenly burst and melted. Tears stung my eyes and I turned away so he couldn't see them.

His hand was gentle on my shoulder. "Don't," he pleaded, "don't try to hide your tears."

"I don't know why I'm crying," I whispered. "Somehow your sensing what I'm trying to communicate means so much."

His voice was low, filled with intensity. "Colleen, I'm glad I came today, saw your painting. Somehow I understand more the person God created you to be. You were right, you know, and I was wrong. You must never let anyone or anything keep you from showing Jesus Christ to the world."

"I love Him so much," I said unsteadily. "But I have so much to learn."

His hand tightened on my shoulder. "You will learn,"

he promised. "I've talked with Alan, Colleen. I hate to admit it, but he's a real man of God."

He turned me to face him and I looked up. Pain and happiness shone together in his dark blue eyes. "This time it really is good-bye," he said quietly.

My own voice was broken. "What about Jill?" I whispered. "Won't you be back to see her?"

"I don't know, but I don't think so. It's too soon." Then he was gone and I drew the silence of the room around me.

Mingled with the loss and pain was a sense of peace. I knew who was the Author of that peace.

Christmas Eve day came and with it another loss.

Sea Biscuit disappeared that day as suddenly as he'd appeared. I searched the town and knocked on doors, anxiously inquiring if anyone had seen him. But no one had seen a rangy yellow dog with a scraggly tail held high.

Tiffany volunteered to accompany me as I roamed farther afield. "But maybe we really shouldn't look," she said. "You always said he'd run away from home. Maybe *he* decided to go back home for Christmas." She looked at me pointedly.

I chose to ignore her implication and stalked on ahead. I almost forgot Sea Biscuit as the sea rushed to meet the dry sand. The scalloped edge of the wave reminded me of a giant flower tossed on the sand, its petals ragged, left too long in the deep, pummeled too long by the wind.

I tried to sketch my fancy into words to Tiffany, but she was curiously detached, disinterested. I stopped in the middle of a sentence and stared at her.

"What's wrong, Tiffany? Is something bothering you?"

The big brown eyes that had been sullenly following the waves' movements suddenly filled with tears. She turned from me and ran toward the town.

I turned and raced after her. "Tiffany! Come back! Come back!" The wind and the sea snatched my words away. She stopped where the sand gave way to rocks and waited. I threw my arms impulsively around her. "Oh, Tiffany!" I gasped. "Don't run from trouble. Let me be with you—help you with what's bothering you."

Tiffany pressed both fists into her eyes. "You can't, Colleen," she wailed.

I hugged her closer. "Try me," I said trying to soothe her.

Tiffany pushed me away and stepped back, dashing tears from angry brown eyes. "It's people!" she cried. "They're mean and unfair!"

She stamped her foot and the rocks rolled beneath her feet. "I don't want you to marry Alan, Colleen. He'll ruin your life—the way Dad has Mom's."

My eyes widened incredulously. "Tiffany, what *are* you talking about? Your parents have a wonderful marriage. And what do Alan and I have to do with it?"

"He's a minister," Tiffany cried. "And ministers have to minister. And so do their wives! And people are always expecting you—do this—and do that—and go here—and not go there!"

"But your parents love it," I protested. "I've never heard them complain—ever."

"Well, I have," Tiffany retorted. "Last night I heard Mother crying. I heard Dad say, 'It means sacrifice, honey. And it means blood and guts and tears. And people will always expect more than you can give. But we give because Jesus gave.' "

Tiffany's foot came down hard on the rocks. "That's not enough, Colleen. It just isn't! I hate Alan. If he really cared about you, he'd let his call be his own. He wouldn't drag you into it."

"But he hasn't tried to drag me into anything, Tiffany. He's not even bothered to call and wish me 'Merry Christmas'!" Even as I said the words something painful tugged inside me. I turned and began to walk up the beach, Tiffany beside me.

"Tiffany, I'm worried about you. You've got to forgive those who've hurt your parents, forget the wrong, or you'll be crippled for life." I thought of Miss Lavender and what she'd endured.

"The pendant!" I exclaimed. "We discovered something, Tiffany!" My voice warmed in my excitement. "It isn't just a pendant, it's a locket. And it carried its own special message to Miss Lavender."

We walked slowly up the beach and I told Tiffany Miss Lavender's story of forgiveness. Even as I told it, I marveled at God's timing.

The sea and the rocks joined their voices to mine as I described the tiny forgiveness stones. The tide rose past the sand onto the rocks, rilling them into music as the waves rushed backward to the sea. Always I knew I would connect that sound with forgiveness—and still another memory, equally as precious—the memory of Tiffany stooping and filling her pockets with smooth stones, stones that would whisper their story of forgiveness to all those to whom she gave them.

"Mrs. Williams," she said slowly, "the Carters, and Alan."

Before we parted, Tiffany slipped her hand in mine. A small smooth pebble pressed into my palm.

"I was angry at you too, Colleen," she whispered. "When you first came I thought you'd be a real friend to my mom. And you have—but then you got so busy with your paintings—with Pete and Alan." She gestured toward the sea. "Even coming here."

A lump rose in my throat. I rolled the round, smooth stone of pearly white in my hand. After that we laughed and hugged as I gave her back her stone.

Then Tiffany and I did something that wasn't a part of Miss Lavender's story. We ran to the top of a sandy mound covered with wild grasses and Tiffany tossed the white stone into the sea. The waves gave great shouts of joy as they swallowed it up. I was sure they clapped their hands.

Tiffany scooted home, but I sat down, my arms clasped around my knees. Words like blood, guts, tears and sacrifice tore through me. Then other words, forgiveness, love, mercy.

In my mind I saw a cross. People—undeserving, harsh people—hating and shouting and crying out in rebellion surged before the cross. And still He died for those unworthy, thankless lives.

The morning sun glowed with a faint glow through the cloud bank behind me. Suddenly a window broke through the clouds. The golden rays slanted toward the water, catching the peaks of the waves in happy light.

I ran to the edge of the waves where the rilling rocks cried out and began to select my own special stones—red for Sherry, green for Melissa, a bluish-gray for Dad. . . .

18 / A Pendant and a Promise

I spent the rest of Christmas Eve day differently than I'd planned. Instead of mooning over Pete's and Sea Biscuit's departure and Alan's neglect, I went to the Mitchell's.

There were dark smudges beneath Sherry's big, dark eyes, and the hollows under her cheekbones were more pronounced than ever as she struggled with Jonathan, unfinished Christmas preparations, and unexpected guests that kept popping in.

Tiffany and I huddled in conference, then burst into action.

Beds were pulled into tiptop shape, the vacuum roared. Tiffany folded newspapers and Christmas wrap, read Jonathan a story and tucked him in for a nap. I cleaned the kitchen then stirred up a batch of brownies to augment Sherry's swiftly diminishing cookie supply.

Evening came and a hush fell over the house.

Sherry caught my arm as I started to slip out the back. "Colleen," she whispered, "I can't begin to thank you."

"Don't try," I said. "We had fun."

"It isn't that." Even in the porch dusk I saw luminous feeling well up in her eyes. She caught my hand in hers. "I think God sent you—or an angel."

"Maybe both?"

"Maybe. I've been feeling so hateful, so—so—needy. And it seemed there was no one I could reach out to—no one." Her eyes burned into my mine.

"God showed me something today, Sherry." I squeezed her hand hard. "It had something to do with you, but mostly it had to do with me. It's difficult to explain but let me try."

Slowly, hesitantly, I shared Amelia and Miss Lavender's story of the forgiveness stones and how it had spoken to my own heart. "For me it has to do with going home—accepting responsibility—not hanging onto my past failures." I furrowed my brows, longing to communicate my heart but not quite knowing how. "It means seeking their forgiveness."

Then I told her of the stones Tiffany and I had gathered, how we'd thrown them into the sea. "I know it sounds childish, Sherry, but it was something we needed to do. I think it was that simple act of obedience that released me—freed me to make the decision to return home. I'm going soon. And I think I'm going to stay."

"Not even if Alan. . . ?" But Sherry didn't finish her thought. Instead she threw her arms around me and held me tight.

"Before you go, can we go to the beach together? I need to gather stones." She laughed shakily. "I need to gather a whole bunch."

"We'll go after Christmas," I agreed. "I won't be going home until . . ." This time it was I who didn't finish my thought. But I didn't need to. Sherry knew what was in my heart.

That evening Miss Lavender and I exchanged gifts in front of the Christmas tree. While I slipped my feet into the warm slipper socks she'd crocheted for me, she exclaimed in delight over the dainty elf maiden combing her hair I had chosen for her.

Then I opened the gifts my family had sent. There was a lacy pullover sweater with silver threads running through powder blue and a matching plaid skirt from Mom and Dad. Melissa had sent a sketchbook, Darryl a set of colored pencils. "So you won't run out of something to do," he wrote in big square writing on the box.

I laughed shakily, wondering if they'd liked the elf sketches, wondering too if Alan had been able to deliver the silver paths. But my real Christmas presents came at the end of the evening. A soft yet urgent scratching at the door brought me to my feet as hope leapt inside me.

"Sea Biscuit!" I cried. I opened the door and he plunged

through it, his yellow tail wagging, his eyes glowing with affection. I dropped to my knees beside him.

"Oh, Sea Biscuit! You naughty prodigal dog! You've come home!"

Then Miss Lavender led me to the telephone. "It's my gift to you. You're to call your family, and talk as long as you want—about anything or nothing."

She left the room and I dialed with hands that weren't quite steady.

"Dad," I whispered. "It's me, Colleen. Guess what? I'm coming home—soon."

My fingers trembled over Sea Biscuit's head as joy boomed over the wire and into my heart. "I knew you were!" he exclaimed. "As soon as I saw those silver paths, I knew what God was trying to tell you."

"Did you like it, really like it?" I asked. "The painting, I mean."

"You've caught something, Colleen. Something deep and real. Yes, I like it. And I like something else. Your young man is someone special, daughter. I can only give you my blessing. . . ."

In the days that followed I hugged his words close to my heart. *Alan,* I thought, *are you feeling what I'm feeling?*

A curious unrest plagued my footsteps and I longed for the peace I'd glimpsed in Jesus only a few days before. *Oh, Alan, if you care,* I thought in the stillness of the night, *why haven't you called? What's happening in your life?*

The questions tumbled around me, dragging me downwards. Then it was almost as though the artistry that flowed from my fingers by day must have another escape.

My thoughts have gone astray, like a little woolly lost sheep. They've wandered on mountain crags, been lost in the forest deep.

Oh, come, kind Shepherd, come. Carry my wandering thoughts home. Anoint their bruises with oil. Teach them no longer to roam.

I took my feelings out and examined them. "I love Alan," I uttered softly under my breath. "But I'm still afraid of responsibility. Alan is so wonderful—has such a ministry ahead of him. Will I ever be able to measure up?''

Later I fell asleep to dream of my Shepherd walking ahead of me along a silver path, His footprints gleaming in front of me. I walked carefully, setting each of my own feet carefully inside the prints. Before I awoke, He turned and took my hand in His—Jehovah Shalom, my God of peace.

December grew old and tired, then faded into January newness.

I stood on the beach on New Year's Eve, exulting in the thought of a year as yet untouched by my hands, wondering what it would bring.

The waves crashed beside me, the wind tore at my scarf and brought stinging sand into my eyes. A solitary surf fisherman yelled, ''Best go in! There's a storm coming!''

I looked in the direction he pointed. Dark angry clouds billowed tall in the south. I shouted my thanks as he hauled in his line, then turned inland.

A white Toyota was sitting in our driveway. I stopped, my stomach plunging treacherously. My knees trembled as I stepped onto the porch and through the kitchen door.

Neither Alan nor Miss Lavender noticed me as they stood together in front of the fireplace, their heads close together. By some quirk of imagination I was plunged into the past.

Lawrence stood by the fireplace and I watched the light gleam off his dark brown hair. Right away I wanted him to notice me, not Opal. She didn't see me at all as I stood outside the kitchen door.

Slowly I backed out the kitchen door. Alan, gone for the holidays, returned, but who was he intent on seeing? Not me! Who did he want to talk with? Miss Lavender! Quite suddenly I was angry at myself and the feelings I'd conjured up inside me.

I ignored the storm building in the south and ran toward the sea. The wind flailed me. I turned north and the wind was behind me shoving me forward, northward.

My chest ached from exertion but still I went forward, jogging before the wind. Once I looked back. The clouds reared dark heads into the sky, menacing me with their darkness and nearness. I shuddered, remembering the storm that had torn my house apart.

But still I ran. In my mind I drew a picture of my Shepherd standing in front of the clouds, one foot planted on the rolling waves, the other on the sand.

My chaotic thoughts quieted, keeping pace with the rhythm of my steps. *Miss Lavender says that peace means wholeness, restoration in relationships—that it's redemption in the fullest sense of the word.*

A wave tossed itself at my feet and I veered around it, amazed at how high on the sand it had come. Then my thoughts returned to the Shepherd, the God of peace, the God of the sea.

Why do I always come to the sea when I'm troubled, I wondered. *Is it because its restlessness matches my own?*

But He's greater than the sea. He knows its paths. He walks upon them. "Thus far," He said to the waves, "you can go, and no farther."

The rocky shore loomed before me, the waves crashing high on the craggy boulders. I leapt onto the lowest rock and watched the water swirl in around it higher and higher, its edges licking at my feet, foam splashing my jeans.

The rock beneath moved and my feet slipped treacherously, tossing me forward. My knee went down hard, smashing onto the rock. Pain lashed me. Another wave slammed close, soaking me to the waist. Sudden fear rose into my throat as I struggled to regain my footing.

It was no use. My foot was tightly wedged between the rocks, and the waves were coming in higher and higher.

"Help!" I cried. "Help!"

The wind grabbed my words and tossed them out to sea. I shoved against the rock with all my strength while the wind screeched its mockery. I battered the rough surface, my fingers growing numb and raw with my futile onslaughts. It was no use. The rock refused to move.

Another wave, driven higher than the one before, broke around me, then swirled back to sea, dragging hard against me. "Help!" I cried, "oh, someone, help!"

The seawater drove into my face, blurring my vision. I closed my eyes. When I opened them I saw a figure, heard a voice. "Colleen! Colleen!"

I tried to answer, but the thundering sea made it impossible for him to hear.

The rock wedging my foot moved and I reached out, clinging to Alan's shoulder. His arm went around me and together we battled the oncoming wave, clutching the rock, hanging tightly against the force of the water.

Then we were free, climbing higher and higher. My legs moved with an effort, a sharp arrow of pain shooting through my foot where the rock had pressed. My knees trembled.

Another wave caught us but we stood still, clinging to each other and the rocky boulders. "Keep climbing!" Alan called as the waves receded.

I did. Even though everything inside me wanted to topple, I hung on step by step, going higher, away from the angry waves, away from the tumult.

We stumbled into the cave, Alan's arm still holding me tight. I was only vaguely aware of a muting of sound as I hid my face into his coat and tried to shut out the storm, the danger we'd walked through together.

I felt both his arms go around me and draw me closer. My own crept around his neck. I lifted my water drenched face to his, saw love and tenderness mirrored in his worried eyes.

"Your foot," he said, his face wreathed in worry. "You were limping. Is it all right?"

I slid my tennis shoe from my foot and probed my foot with my fingertips. "Just bruised I think."

I lifted my hand and tenderly touched the worry crinkle between his brows. A great longing rose inside me. If only I could wipe it away—forever.

"I love you," he whispered. "Oh, Colleen, when I saw you pinned tight by that rock, I knew I wanted to spend my life with you—all of it."

Then he kissed me. Afterward I clung to him, delighting

in the feel of his cheek against my own, taking comfort in the pressure of his arms strong and tight around me.

We sat down on a boulder close together. It didn't matter that our clothes were wet and stiff with seawater, that our hair was wind-tossed and unruly. The cave put its arms around us, protecting us from the force of the wind.

"I love you, Alan," I said unsteadily, "but I've been so afraid—of responsibility. So many things—"

"I know," he said tenderly.

I leaned my head wearily against his shoulder. "Today I discovered something about myself, Alan. When I was running with the storm," I began, taking a long, jagged breath, "I suddenly knew why I always went to the ocean when I was mixed up, troubled, afraid. It's because the restlessness of the sea matched the restlessness in me."

"But," Alan protested, "that's not right—"

"Wait. Let me explain. All this time," I gestured toward the sea, "and even before, I've fought against the Lord's claim on my life. Oh, I know I've been learning—through Jack's ministry, Amelia's diary, God's Word, even through my new paintings. But until now I haven't really reached out and grasped His peace—the peace of total commitment. I'm still grasping."

I buried my face in my hands, searching for words to communicate what was in my heart. Then I turned to him. "I love you," I said, "but I have to go home. I've already decided. And it isn't just for a visit. It will be to stay a while. You see, this new peace my Shepherd is offering me has to come out in obedience, or it isn't real!"

"I know," he said quietly. "I know."

"I'm not sure if you really do." I struggled for words. "It's only as I obey Him in this first baby step that I'll be able to obey in the second step."

"And that is?"

"My fear of responsibility—the inadequacies I have of becoming the wife of a man whom I sense God is going to use mightily. That is, if you're asking me—"

He drew me to him. Our lips met and clung.

"My beloved, my wife. We'll take that second step when the time comes."

My eyes stung with tears. He reached up, tenderly brushing the one that overflowed onto my cheek. "I'll wait," he said reverently, "the rest of my life if I have to."

"No!" I protested. "I want to belong to you—soon." Sudden shyness tangled my tongue. "I—I talked to Daddy about you. He said—he said, 'I can only give you my blessing.' "

Alan reached into his pocket. "Shut your eyes."

Something cool and smooth slipped around my neck. My hand reached up. "Amelia's necklace!" I whispered wonderingly. I opened my eyes and caressed the moon pendant. "But Alan, why—how?"

"It's my pledge that I'm committed to you forever."

"But I don't understand!" I cried. "Why is Miss Lavender's pendant yours to give?"

Then while the storm blew itself out across the rocks, Alan told me his grandfather's story. Together we stole back into time . . .

"It began when Granddad told me he'd left something precious at Driftwood Beach," Alan said. "I thought he meant just memories.

"Then—do you remember the day I brought back the pendant? I didn't tell you at that time, but I found something inside besides the tiny forgiveness stone. A picture."

He smiled. "You always said you liked me with a beard. Well, you would have liked that tiny picture inside. I couldn't believe it when I saw it." He shook his head. "It was so like me. When I showed it to Miss Lavender, she recognized Lawrence Redgate right away."

I gasped. "And she'd never seen you with a beard."

"I know. She'd never made the connection that Amelia's long lost lover was Lawrence Redgrave, my grandfather—who, believe it or not, looks incredibly like me."

"What a strange coincidence," I marveled. "Strange . . ."

"Not really. With God there are never coincidences, just

good planning—His planning.''

"I know," I sighed. "But Alan, their story—Lawrence and Amelia's—even Miss Lavender's—is so sad.''

I bent my head forward. "Would you unsnap it, Alan? I want to look at it.''

It lay in my hand, a symbol of love and forgiveness. Alan leaned over and opened the locket in my palm. The bearded face, so much like Alan's, looked out at me.

"I told him about you, Colleen. He was delighted. He wanted you to have the pendant as a pledge of our commitment to each other.''

I smiled at Lawrence Redgate, then closed the locket, holding it against my cheek. "I think our story will be different, Alan. Because it will be built on a rock—Christ Jesus.''

I looked at the rocky outcropping over me, revelled again in the way it kept the storm at bay. "No—more than a rock. He's my Shepherd, the God of Peace, the Shepherd of the sea who came to me—who goes before me, even now, leading me home.''

Once again Alan took me in his arms. "For you shall go out with joy," he promised, "and be led forth with peace; the mountains and hills shall break forth before you into singing, and all the trees of the field shall clap their hands!''

Springflower Books (for girls 12–15):

Melissa
Michelle
Lisa
Sara
Erica

Heartsong Books (for young adults):

Kara
Jenny
Andrea
Anne
Karen
Carrie
Colleen